Mommy, Can You Feel Me?

By

Vickie J Blair

ISBN-13:978-1500151850
ISBN-10:1500151858

Contact Information:
P.O. Box 6737
Banks, AL 36005
USA

Email:vjbprojectk@gmail.com

Vickie's Blog

www.vickiejblair.com

For women everywhere
who have experienced
or
who are currently debating
the issue of abortion.

May you be blessed and find the
road to peace.

This is also for parents
who are burdened for their children who
are not interested in the things of God.
May you find encouragement and hope in
these pages.

ACKNOWLEDGEMENTS

*My dear friend, Chris Gracen Reeves, has done it again! She has devoted valuable time to dissect my words, adding clarity and grammatical correction. As always, thank you Chris for what you have done. I write that with a heart overflowing in appreciation.

*I also wish to thank Bronwen Pearson, a highly qualified and experienced counsellor in the UK, who has assisted women facing pregnancy issues for many years. Thank you, Bronwen, for your perusing of my research concerning the medical matters touched on in this book.

A note to the reader: As with every manuscript, the final editing choices are my own. Therefore, if you find any mistakes, those are mine, too.

6

TABLE OF CONTENTS

THE REQUEST

"Jesus, can I send my Mommy a message?"

"A message, little one? That's not how we normally do things here."

"I know, but I thought it might help my Mommy. Maybe it will help other Mommies, too."

"Write your message and give it to me."

The little one wrote out a message and gave it to Jesus. Jesus then called an angel who came right away.

"Take this message to earth," Jesus said. "It's urgent."

The angel did as he was commanded. He quickly located the one for whom the message was written. He lay the letter on her bedside table, shook her lightly until she woke up, then disappeared from sight.

The woman yawned and stretched, enjoying the snuggly feeling of the warmth of her bed. The soft blankets enveloped her. She pulled and tucked them even tighter beneath her chin. She would get up — soon. Just a few more minutes of resting, she thought to herself, as she opened one eye to glance at the clock. But, what was that? She woke up fully now, her senses awakened by her curiosity.

There, next to the clock, was a white envelope. It had her name on it. She glanced around the room. Who could have put it there? Feeling somewhat alarmed, she jumped out of bed, all thoughts of being warm and snuggly gone out the window.

She deftly slipped on her robe, picked up a high heel, and brandishing it like a weapon proceeded cautiously through the house. Was someone hiding? Was someone playing a trick on her? Whoever it was, this was not funny! She went from one room to the other checking all closets and looking under the furniture. There was no one there. Her doors were still locked as she had left them the night before. There was no sign of entry from anyone.

She felt relieved, but only for a moment. Her fear struck another chord as she thought of the note on her bedside table. Did she dream it all? She went back into her bedroom. The white envelope with her name on it still lay where she had seen it. Curiosity made her want to read it immediately; fear made her less than anxious to touch it.

She decided she would dress for the day and pour her ritual cup of coffee to get the inner juices moving. Only then would she sit down and read whatever it was that was in the mysterious envelope.

Taking a welcomed sip of the soothing, hot liquid, she slit open the envelope and looked inside. It was filled with several pages. Who put this here? she mused to herself, glancing around again just to make certain no one was lurking in her house after all.

She unfolded the white pages; white like snow, she thought. The paper was thick and soft to the touch. Very expensive, her thought lines continued as she held the pages open and began to read.

"Hi Mommy, it's me, your baby."

The woman gasped. Looking around the room again she was filled with fear, then rage! Who would do such a cruel thing? She was vexed at the imaginings that swept through her mind. Who would be so cruel?

She sat for a long time, her knees drawn up with her chin resting on them. Her arms were wrapped around her legs and her eyes were staring, then darting around, then staring again. Who has done this? Her mind whirled in myriads of emotion. She was angry at whomever had sent this note. She was afraid to think someone came into her home without detection. Then, she admitted, she was filled with a sorrow, perhaps even with some guilt.

Her once welcomed cup of coffee had grown cold. She got up to pour it down the sink. Should she make another cup? No, she didn't want anything. Should she read the letter? No, it would only upset her even more. But where did it come from? She could feel herself being drawn back to the envelope with its thick pages of white laying on top of it. Curiosity would win, she knew it, and so she resolved to sit down, read the letter, and get it over with. She would deal with whomever the prankster was as soon as she could find out who did this awful thing.

THE MESSAGE

"Mommy, I asked Jesus if I could write to you. I wanted to explain something."

The woman took her eyes off the page. Her heart was racing. She couldn't breathe! Inhale slowly and deeply, she instructed herself, slowly and deeply. She no longer felt fearful or even angry. She felt — she didn't know how she felt. Could this really be happening?

She thought back to days when she attended church. It was only once in a while and only to placate those in her life who considered going to church a good thing to do. If it made her family and some of her friends happy, then why not? Church might not help, but it couldn't hurt, so she attended often enough to appease but not so much that it became an aggravation to her. After all, she didn't want to ruin every Sunday with going to church! She had a life to live.

She looked back to the page she was still holding in her hands. Determinedly she forced her eyes to focus on the next words. "I want you to know that I'm happy here with Jesus, even though I was so looking forward to being with you. I remember so much and, Mommy, I've learned so much more since coming to be with Jesus. Do you want to know what I learned, Mommy? Do you want to know what was happening to me when I was in your tummy house?"

Tummy house! The woman's mind was racing again, heart palpitating in heavy beats like a drum in her chest. Surely this was not referring to *that* exact time! Was it? Wiping her brow with a tissue, she continued.

"It all started with the holy record. You know what it says about me, Mommy? Here it is, the beginning parts of the Holy Record. Look what it says, Mommy." The woman's eyes read down the page, taking in the words that were recorded as 'The Holy Record.' This is what is said:

THE HOLY RECORD

Recorded in Heaven - Day One

Egg and sperm merging. Life granted. From this point Psalm 139:13-16 set in motion: "*You made all the delicate, inner parts of my body and knit me together in my mother's womb. Thank you for making me so wonderfully complex! Your workmanship is a marvel — and how well I know it. You watched me as I was being formed in utter seclusion, as I was woven together in the dark of the womb, You saw me before I was born. Every day of my life was recorded in your book. Every moment was laid out before a single day had passed.*"

Weeks 1 - 3
Cells are arranging themselves to form all the parts of the baby.

Weeks 4 - 5
Three layers of cells have formed together to create the organs and other body parts.

"Hi Mommy, it's me again. Isn't it real cool that there's a holy record about me? There's one about you, too, Mommy. Everyone has a record. When I read my record for the first time, I got real excited, especially with the start of week six, so I'll tell you about the record now, ok, Mommy?"

The woman was breathing in short, fast breaths. Could she continue this? No! Yes! Who did this? Her eyes were drawn to the words like a magnet to metal. She could not remove her gaze.

"Did you know that in week six my arms and legs were coming, sort of like little buds, and my hands and feet looked like little paddles? I could move those little paddles. Did you know that, Mommy? And guess what else? My mouth was getting a tongue inside and my vocal chords were forming! That's what makes it so we can talk. You probably know that already. That's not all! Did you know that my heart started beating this week?"

"Oh!" The woman threw aside the pages, pulled a tissue out of her pocket, and pressed it tight against her eyes. Then she bent forward and began to cry. The tears quickly turned to sobbing. She was weeping so heavily that her breath was caught away. She choked and wept for many more minutes before her shaking shoulders finally settled into stillness and her breathing became easy again.

My baby's heart was beating? She held her breath for a moment to still the tears that were ready to burst forth once more. But — but it's not a life until it's born, she argued with herself. But what makes a life? Can something not yet alive have a beating heart? Her contemplations took her deeper inside herself to a place she didn't want to go. Quit thinking! She shouted at her brain, then fell back on the couch in her confusion. She didn't want to think anymore, but the thoughts took on a will of their own. When does death come? she asked herself. "When someone's heart stops," she said aloud, almost in a whisper.

The choking began all over again, mixed with more tears and more shoulder shaking. Is this true? Is this true? She ran to the toilet, feeling as if she might be sick. She stayed bent over the toilet for several minutes until the wave of nausea eased away. Splashing cold water on her face and neck, she wanted this day to be over. She wanted to go back to bed, go to sleep, and wake up with everything different.

She stared in the mirror. What is happening to me? Someone has been cruel. Maybe I should phone someone. My mother? No, she would probably claim it as a sign from God. A neighbor? A friend? No, there was actually no one she wanted to talk to right now. She knew why. It was like that envelope with its pages were calling to her. She was compelled to return and read on.

"During week seven," she began to read, "I had eyelids and they were covering my eyes. Guess what else, Mommy? My intestines were growing. I've learned all about intestines up here, Mommy. They're amazing! Did you know that our intestines get to be 25 feet long? I laughed when I learned that, Mommy. I told Jesus it reminded me of spaghetti, and He laughed, too. Jesus laughs a lot, and He likes playing with all the children. Are you surprised I know about spaghetti? I told you, Mommy, I've learned lots and lots here in heaven."

The woman smiled for the first time since she found the envelope. Spaghetti. That's my favorite food, she mused. I wonder if there's spaghetti in heaven. She then shook her head as if trying to clear the fog and shake sense into her thoughts.

"Mommy," she continued reading, "in week eight guess what happened to me? Nerve cells were branching out to form neural pathways. Do I sound like a scientist, Mommy? Neural pathways! Jesus told me about neural pathways. They're like roads in our bodies that send messages to our brain."

What? I can't do this. The woman laid the pages aside and went to the kitchen. Another cup of coffee, that's what she needed. Why, she didn't even have her first cup. It went all cold. Yes, a cup of coffee. She put the kettle on to boil, leaned back against the counter, and stared into her backyard.

Could this really be a message from heaven? Why, things like that don't happen. Of course not! Someone's joke or perhaps someone's way of making a point? Her mind raced, first picturing her friends and their viewpoints. She then widened her circle to her work colleagues. Had she ever discussed the beginning and ending of life with them? Had she told them what she had done? A few of her friends knew. Some agreed. Others didn't, but that was just a matter of opinion, wasn't it? There's not really a right or wrong answer, is there?

The kettle was whistling now. She moved to the stove, poured hot water into her waiting cup, took a whiff of the coffee, and returned to the couch. The pages were strewn to one side. She collected them together and began to read again.

"Mommy, aren't ears funny? I don't know why I think they're funny but they make me laugh. I got my ear lobes at week nine. Guess what else? I got my own fingerprints! They're different from your fingerprints. Everybody has their own, everybody in the whole world! Isn't that amazing, Mommy? Jesus gave us all different fingerprints just to let us know that we're each one special to Him."

Fingerprints. Still holding the pages, the woman rested her hands in her lap and stared into nothingness again. Then she lifted one hand and looked at the tips of her fingers. She got those when she was just nine weeks old? Everybody gets their own fingerprints when they're just nine weeks old? Tears filled her eyes yet again. She just sat still, letting them roll down her face and drip off her chin.

I never looked at it this way before. I didn't know the heart beats at six weeks and fingerprints are formed at nine weeks. I didn't know. I just thought that some people, pro-life people, were old fashioned, stuck in a self-righteous rut, going around judging others.

Suddenly, she wanted to go online and look up pictures of a fetus and the different stages that happen before birth, but she couldn't. No, I'm not ready for that yet. I have to think. I have to get things straight in my mind. Is all this true? Someone is just trying to make me feel guilty! I have a right to make decisions about my own body! It's my right! I don't want to read this anymore. But she did.

"Guess what else happened that week, Mommy? Did you feel anything bumping around? Ha Ha — that was me! It was so much fun. I could bend and stretch my legs and arms. I wanted you to know, Mommy, so I put my feet against the wall of my tummy house, and I pushed hard! Did you feel me, Mommy?"

Oh, dear God! The woman dropped the pages to the floor. She stood. Then she sat down again. Then she stood. She paced. She wanted to think. She didn't want to think. When would this all end? I need a break.

She grabbed her purse and car keys and headed out the door. She drove robotically. She went out onto the highway, turning down smaller roads she had never been down before. She didn't know where she was going, nor did she care. She just drove. This went on for a couple of hours until her car accidentally found itself back on the same highway she started out on, only several miles away. She turned the car in the direction of home, but thirty minutes later she was pulling into the parking lot of a building with a sign that read Planned Parenthood Women's Center.

PRO-CHOICE DISCUSSION

"Well, hello again." The receptionist greeted the woman with a friendly smile.

"You remember me?"

"I certainly do." The receptionist stood and moved to the counter that separated the two women. "What can I do for you?"

"Well, I — I— oh, I suddenly feel silly."

"Try not to. You know we are here to help. Would you like me to get someone to talk with you?"

"Oh, yes, thank you. I would like that. I know I don't have an appointment."

"That's no problem. Have a seat and I'll get someone for you. Can I get you a cup of tea or coffee?"

"Oh, no, but thank you."

The receptionist sat back down, pushed a button and began to talk, asking if someone was free to talk with a woman who had just arrived. Replacing the phone receiver into its cradle, the receptionist smiled again and said, "Someone will be right with you."

"Thank you."

"No problem." The smiling receptionist returned to the screen of her computer and began typing.

The woman glanced around the pleasant room. She remembered her last visit here. Everyone was always so nice and helpful and reassuring. That's what she needed now — reassurance. Yes. She would talk to someone in the know, and they would unscramble her present thoughts. Then she would go home and carry on as normal.

"Well hello, it's nice to see you again." Another woman, dressed in a tailored skirt and jacket, walked forward with her arm outstretched. The woman stood and took hold of the hand offered to her. A firm and welcome clasp wrapped around her fingers.

"Come this way. Would you like some tea or coffee?"

"No, thank you," the woman answered.

She was led to a small but cheerful room. There were three armchairs, each with an end table decorated with vases of silk flowers. The colors in the upholstery and the curtains were in shades of mauve and deep blues. The woman had not been in this room before. She took a seat.

Still smiling, the other woman said, "You might remember, I'm one of the counselors here."

"Yes, I do remember, and I'm very impressed that all of you seem to remember me, too. I know you have lots of people that come through those doors."

"We do, but we make a point to try and remember names and faces. It's important to us that everyone who walks through those doors knows they're not just a number or a name on a form.

We're truly here to be of help during what can be a very difficult time."

The woman sensed her sincerity. "Do you have children?" she asked, then immediately regretted her question. "Oh, I do apologize, that is not for me to know."

"It's a natural question to ask. I don't mind. You're not the first to ask me. Yes, I have two daughters."

"You never thought of not having them?"

"No. Both my pregnancies came at times in mine and my partner's lives where having children was going to be a joy rather than the hardship that many women would find them to be."

"Yes," the woman stared at the floral patterns on the curtains before saying, "If you don't mind me asking, what are some of the hardships that women face with unwanted pregnancies? I mean, what makes them unwanted? Oh! I'm not explaining myself very well."

"You're doing fine." The counselor was indeed kind and patient. The woman was so thankful that she wasn't made to feel a bother or in the way for any reason.

"Hardships that women face." The counselor sat back in her chair as she answered, "A woman may have had the physical and emotional trauma of having been raped."

The woman nodded. Yes, that would certainly be hard to have the child of a rapist. It was like the counselor had read her mind as she said, "Some women find it too emotionally stressful to think of mothering a child whose father is a rapist."

"What else?" The woman asked.

"Sometimes a woman discovers that her fetus has Down's syndrome or has another physical challenge that would be difficult to handle."

The woman frowned as she responded. "My mother has a close friend who gave birth to a Down's syndrome child. The parents were saddened, of course, but well — I've met the child and she's absolutely lovely. She goes to school, reads, writes. And she even helps at a local gardening store. The parents lost their sadness long ago. I suppose it was just the shock, at first, and not knowing how things were going to be." The woman chuckled as she said further, "They're certainly not sad anymore. They're so proud of her accomplishments, and she's really got a great sense of humor. Like I said, she's a lovely girl."

The counselor leaned forward as she said, "It was the parent's choice to make the best of their situation, and it sounds as if they have done just that. I'm glad to hear it. I'm glad for all of them. It's their choice. For others, to have had such a choice forced on them would have proved to be a nightmare."

"Why?" The woman asked and quickly added. "I'm just trying to understand."

The counselor, with her eternal kind smile, leaned forward and asked gently, "May I ask, are you pregnant again?"

"Oh, no. No, really, I'm not." She paused as a sudden rush of embarrassment washed over her. "Oh, dear, this must all seem crazy."

"Why don't you tell me exactly why you're here," the counselor urged, "then we can get right to the problem and the solution." The woman nodded. Of course. That was the only right thing to do. She must quit beating around the bush and get right to the point of her visit.

"How long since your abortion?" The counselor looked at the ceiling as if the answer might be written there. "Three or four months, is it?"

"Four," the woman said.

"And now, you're — regretting?"

"Oh, you are good at your job," the woman answered with relief, glad that she didn't have to explain further.

"Excuse me for just a moment," the counselor said as she stood to leave the room. "I'll be right back. I want to show you something. Sure you don't want any coffee or tea?"

"I'm sure, thank you."

The woman felt more relaxed. She was glad she came. This would help her to get her thoughts straight again. Everything was suddenly so scrambled in her brain. Soon she would feel at ease. She settled back in her chair to wait for the counselor to return. The door opened.

"I want to read something to you," the counselor said as she sat down and opened a folder. As she was flipping through pages she said, "There are many people who believe abortion to be a moral issue. For some, that is the case, but that can't be inferred upon every person. For example, it may be a moral issue for those who follow a religion. However, those who have no religion have a different viewpoint on morality."

Wow, the woman surmised, this counselor really knows her stuff. I'm so glad I came. She felt her lips form a smile as she continued to listen. The counselor went on.

"Regardless of whether or not one considers the matter to be a moral issue, one thing is certain. It is a constitutional issue. It is by the guarantee of our constitution the right of a woman to choose what she does with her body. This right to choose should not be altered by anyone else's opinion. Let me read the ninth amendment* of our constitution to you: 'The enumeration in the Constitution, of certain rights, shall not be construed to deny or disparage others retained by the people'."

The woman's face contorted. I'm sorry," she laughed nervously, to her chagrin, "but I don't understand what in the world that amendment is saying."

The counselor laughed too, and true to form, she quickly put the woman at rest. "I know! Law jargon! I didn't understand it either at one time." Crossing her legs and leaning forward she said simply, "It means that you — anyone — has the right by law to make decisions concerning your own body."

* US Bill of Rights, Ninth Amendment, referenced in *Roe vs. Wade, 1973*

The woman said nothing as she tried to understand. The counselor flipped a few more pages in her folder and then explained, "Ah! Here's what I've been looking for; I kept flipping over it without seeing it." She laughed at herself, then her tone took on a serious note as she said, "Regardless of morals, a woman has the right to privacy and a right to abort her fetus. The people that hold a "pro-life" view argue that a woman who has an abortion is killing a child. The "pro-choice" perspective holds that this is not the case. Why?"

The woman wondered if she was supposed to answer. Her throat tightened but relaxed again when the counselor answered the question herself. "Because a fetus is not yet a baby." She smiled wide with this announcement as if this one sentence gave all the answer needed. Keeping her eyes on the woman she added with obvious excitement, "We know it's not a baby yet because it does not meet the criteria derived from our understanding of what makes a living, human being."

"I hear what you are saying," the woman began, "but I don't understand how we've come to the conclusion that a fetus isn't a baby. What criteria are you talking about?"

"That's what I'm coming to," the counselor answered, still holding that huge smile as if she held the best answer in the world. The woman hoped she did. She wanted to know that a fetus is not a baby. She wanted to know of a certainty so she could go home, throw that letter away, and get on with her life.

"There is a respected philosopher, Mary Anne Warren, who has given a most notable explanation concerning the life of a human being. She wrote her conclusions in a book entitled *Biomedical Ethics.* She calls life in this instance — personhood. This is how she defines personhood:*

* Warren, Mary Anne. *Biomedical Ethics* 4th ed. pp. 434-440

'1) consciousness (of objects and events external and or internal to the being), and in particular the capacity to feel pain

2) reasoning (the developed capacity to solve new and relatively complex problems)

3) self-motivated activity (activity which is relatively independent of either genetic or direct external control)

4) the capacity to communicate, by whatever means, messages of an indefinite variety of types, that is, not just with an indefinite number of possible contents, but on indefinitely many possible topics

5) the presence of self-concepts, and self-awareness, either individual or social, or both.'"

The counselor closed the folder with a snap of triumph. The eternal smile was radiant. She re-crossed her legs, settled back in the chair, and asked, "Well?"

The woman knew she was supposed to say something like, "Oh yes, that's all clear." In part it was, but there was something still bothering her deep inside. She couldn't even form the words to explain her feelings to herself, much less to the smiling counselor beaming in front of her.

Clearing her throat, really as a way to stall for time and giving herself needed moments to think of something to say, she repositioned herself in her chair. She then asked, "Could I possibly have a copy of that?"

The counselor's smile broadened even more; something that the woman would not have thought possible. "You certainly can. I'll be right back." The counselor left the room to get a copy.

The woman stood and walked over to the window. The blinds were closed, she supposed, for privacy. She turned as the door opened again.

"Oh, that was quick," she said.

"We keep copies on hand." She held the copy out to the woman as she asked, "Is there anything more I can help you with?"

"No, not now, but you've been so helpful. I thank you for your time, especially as I just sort of burst in."

The counselor laughed kindly and replied, "Not at all. You come anytime you need to talk. It's why we're here."

THE MESSAGE CONTINUES

Back in her car, the woman headed home and made it to her door this time. As she pulled onto her driveway, she sat for some minutes just thinking. In one way, she wanted to go inside and continue reading more of the contents of that white envelope. Another part of her wanted to go inside and discover they had disappeared.

When she did go inside, the pages were still right where she had left them. She sighed and thought of that cup of coffee she had yet to drink, but this time abandoned even the attempt. Instead, punching a couch cushion into shape, she leaned back against it, picked up the pages, and began reading again.

"Mommy," she read, and this time felt a slight tugging at the corners of her mouth — a smile trying to form. She was becoming familiar with this person calling her Mommy. Wait! No! This wasn't a person writing; it was all a hoax! She needed to find out who had written it. But what if it wasn't a hoax?

Taking a deep breath to help force her arguing thoughts from her mind, she held the page before her and read the words written there. "Mommy, the very next week my fingers were all separated, and I had fingernails."

"You know what happened over the next three weeks? My eyes and ears were in their final places. I think I have ears like you, Mommy. My arms and legs were longer. My lungs were developing air sacs. That's so I could breathe when I came out of my tummy house. I was getting all ready to live with you, Mommy."

The woman needed another break. She pulled a tissue from the box on the table by the couch and dabbed at her eyes once again. They were very sore from the wash of tears that had been flowing since daybreak.

She should eat something. No, I'm not hungry at all, but I should eat something.

It won't help matters if I get a headache from not eating.

She got up, walked into the kitchen, and took turns staring into the cupboards and then into the refrigerator. Back and forth, back and forth she looked. The cupboards and fridge were packed with food, but with nothing she wanted.

Finally, she selected a brown bread roll and some leftover tuna salad from the day before. She smeared on mayonnaise, and then spread the tuna onto the roll. She took a bite. It was delicious yesterday; today it was a real effort to swallow. Even so, after some long minutes, she managed to consume the tasteless food on her plate.

She sat some more long minutes staring out into the backyard. She finished the glass of orange juice that she had also made herself swallow, in spite of no enjoyment; then she resumed the compelling task of reading the pages on the couch in her living room.

"Mommy, this is amazing! At only sixteen weeks my heart was pumping 25 quarts of blood — everyday! Are you amazed, Mommy? I knew you would be. That's not all —"

"It has to be all! I can't take anymore!" The woman shouted out in agony, once again wiping her stinging, inflamed eyes. If only she could dab at her hurting heart, to soothe it of some of its pain, but she could not. There was no consolation to alleviate the turmoil that had taken hold of her innermost being. The fingers of emotional torture would not let go.

Sleep. She had to sleep. She went to her bedroom, eased beneath the covers, and to her surprise but relief, she felt her body growing heavy as it yielded to slumber.

Did she dream or have a nightmare? She saw herself walking with a little girl. They were laughing. They were happy. Then, a dark hole appeared and the little girl was swirling in fast circles, sucked into the hole as into a flushing toilet.

"Uhhh!" The woman sat straight up, her hair scattered over her face. She was breathing in short puffs. She sat motionless for many minutes, frozen in the fear of her agitating thoughts.

Automatically, she pushed the bed cover off, walked into the living room, picked up the pages, perched herself on the edge of the couch cushion, and read again. Her hair looked like a bird's nest. Her mouth twisted in distress. Her blank red eyes showed her haunted bewilderment. Why was this happening to her?

"Mommy, did you know that when I first came into my tummy house that I was all rubbery? Isn't that funny? Jesus said that's because I was forming fast and it was easier to keep me rubber. Ha ha. I laugh every time I think about being a rubber baby! Ha ha ha."

A rubber baby. The woman smiled just a little, although her anguish continued.

"Mommy, when I was just nineteen weeks old, I could smell, taste, hear, see, and feel things. Isn't that amazing? Oh, I almost forgot to tell you — sometimes my eyes hurt a little, but that was okay, Mommy, I just turned over in my tummy house. I asked Jesus why my eyes hurt. You know what He said, Mommy? This is funny, too. He said you were taking a sunbath and the light was so bright it hurt my eyes. A sun bath! Mommy, that's so funny! You're supposed to have a water bath. Ha ha ha. I'm just joking, Mommy."

The woman let out a long sigh. Her limp arms barely held the pages, which were now dangling from fingers, precariously hanging over the edge of the couch cushion. The pages slid to the floor. The woman lay over on her side. She did not cry. After many minutes she realized she was absently staring at the coffee table leg.

"Get up." The woman whispered the command. "Get up." Her body refused to obey until an unexpected idea jumped into her bewildered brain. Call your mother. The woman's eyes opened wide in astonishment. Call my mother? Yes! Yes, I will. I will call my mother.

The woman and her mother had not been on the best of terms for some time. Her mother was a church goer. She was not. This put them at odds, at least it did so in the woman's mind.

Actually, her mother never nagged. The woman smiled as she thought of her mother — always there when she needed her. The problem can't be my mother, the woman's heart spoke to her head. It's me. It's my own sense of guilt at ignoring my childhood love of — No! She did not continue her thoughts. I have enough thinking to do! Enough!

She sat longer and felt her body relax again. Once more the thought to call her mother came to her. She leaned forward, pulled a cell phone out of her purse, and scrolled until her mother's name appeared on the screen. She tapped the number and waited for her mother's voice to sound in her ear.

"Hello?"

"Hi, Mom."

"Hi Hon, Dad and I were just thinking about you."

"You were?" The woman was suddenly nervous. Had they received a similar message? Had someone played a cruel joke on them, too?

"Yes," her mother continued with a jovial lilt to her voice, "I'm just preparing chicken to fry, crispy the way you like it. We'll be sitting down to a late lunch or a very early dinner, whatever you want to call it. Come on over!" Her mother's voice was friendly, loving, inviting.

"I — I can't now, Mom, I —"

"Mashed potatoes and gravy, too!" Her mother tried to tempt her.

"No, I really can't." She hesitated and her mother asked, "Are you okay, Hon?"

"Mom, I was wondering — could you — do you think that I — could I have your pastor's phone number? Do you think he would mind if I phoned him?"

Her mother lifted her eyes heavenward and said a silent thank you in her heart, then answered with a lighthearted, "I have the number right here and no, our pastor won't mind you phoning him." She asked no questions; she was just thankful beyond words that her daughter was actually going to phone a pastor.

Her mother called out the number. "Did you get it?" Her daughter repeated it back to her. "That's right. Now, that's the office number. Let me give you his home number, too, just in case." She called out the number. Her daughter repeated it, thanked her mother, and hung up.

Now that she had the number, what would she say to the pastor? What should she say to the receptionist at the church when she phoned? She hoped she wouldn't have to give a reason for her call; it was personal. No, she told herself, they are a church. They're used to people coming in for personal reasons. I'm sure they'll not press me for information I don't want to give.

She sat on the couch, then moved to sit at the dining table. Then she walked back to the couch. What am I doing? Phone! She tapped the number to the church. A friendly voice answered, giving the name of the church and asking, "May I help you?"

"I was just wondering," the woman heard words coming from her mouth, but felt like it was someone else. What a strange feeling, she mused, as she continued with, "could I make an appointment to speak with the pastor?"

"Certainly, could I have your name?"

The woman gave her name and felt herself cringing with the thought of being asked what she wanted to talk about. Her cringing eased when the woman asked, "How soon would you hope to speak with him?"

"Oh, well, I'm sure he's always busy. I —"

"Would you like to come in this afternoon?" the friendly voice asked. "He'll be back in his office soon, and I can see that his appointments calendar is free for the rest of the afternoon. Is today too soon?"

The woman could hardly believe her luck. She heard herself saying, "Oh, that would be great! Thank you. I'll come anytime at all."

"Well," the receptionist said, "can you be here in 45 minutes?"

"Yes, I don't live far away."

"Good. The pastor is just finishing a late lunch, so 45 minutes from now will be perfect. We'll look forward to seeing you then."

"Thank you. Thank you, very much."

"Our pleasure," said the friendly voice. She hung up.

Lunch. The pastor is having lunch. It's 3:30. I guess a pastor's timetable is very flexible with all the people he cares for and sermons he has to prepare and people to visit in the hospital, she thought, and those deacon's meetings. She actually smiled as she remembered her father coming home from deacon's meetings.

"If we deacons could agree the first time on anything," he would say in mock irritation, "we would all pass out with heart attacks."

"Well, then," her mother would join in on the pretense, "how wonderful you can't agree hurriedly; the church would be full of widows."

It was the same joke said after every deacon's meeting, the same response from her mother, and the same hugs between them afterwards. She had come from a happy home.

What happened? She knew what happened. No time to think about that now; she had other things more pressing on her mind. The hoax — or — maybe not a hoax. What would the pastor say?

She walked into the bathroom and regaining composure after looking at her disheveled self in the mirror gathered her make-up and hair brush. "Time for repair work," she said aloud.

In fifteen minutes she was in her car, surprised at her feelings of calm. Good, she told herself. I need some calm at last in my day. She drove to the church, pulling into the parking lot with five minutes to spare. Glancing in the mirror, she decided that she was presentable in spite of swollen, red eyes.

A sudden panic hit her. Open the door and get out. No! Forget the whole thing! I can't forget — that's why I'm here! Get out of the car! Go home! No!

"Hello," the receptionist was smiling as she came in the door. "The pastor knows you are coming. He said to show you right in when you arrived." The receptionist stood and walked to a door at the far end of the squared reception area. The woman followed, noting the green plants, soft music, and the overall peaceful atmosphere. She felt herself let out a breath of relief.

The receptionist knocked lightly on the door. "Come in," called a voice on the other side. Opening the door the receptionist said, "Your next appointment is here." Smiling, she held the door open for the woman and closed it behind her after the woman had walked in.

THE ROAD OF DISCOVERY

"Hello!"

The pastor came out from behind his desk with his hand extended. She took it and felt his warm grasp shake her hand.

"Please, have a seat," he said, indicating one of two chairs that were positioned in front of his desk. He went back around the desk and took his own chair.

Leaning forward he said, "I know your parents well."

"Yes — I — I wondered if I should tell you who I am, but you've already figured that out." The woman was slightly annoyed. Had her mother phoned to say she had asked for his number?

"I wasn't certain. I just made an educated guess." He was smiling as he continued. "Your parents have told me they have a daughter and have always referred to you by name. When my receptionist wrote your name down on my appointments calendar — well — I took a wild guess." He chuckled as if he had just said something really funny.

The woman relaxed and felt a little ashamed. Why was she always thinking the worst about her mother? Her mother wouldn't know she had actually phoned and certainly wouldn't know she was right now sitting in the pastor's office. She must quit thinking the worst.

Oh, no! The pastor had been talking to her and she was in dreamland! What had he said to her? He was still leaning forward, smiling, waiting for her to respond to — what? Had he made a comment or asked a question? Oh, how embarrassing! Why am I here?

"If you don't mind me saying so, I don't want to be presumptuous, but you seem distracted, possibly by something troubling you?" The pastor leaned back in his chair now and waited for the woman sitting before him to respond. She did. Tears filled her eyes. She began wiping them away.

"Here." The pastor had opened a desk drawer and took out a box of tissues. He placed them in front of her. She was grateful but embarrassed again.

"I'm so sorry," she began apologetically.

"Please don't be," the kind pastor said. His words were gentle and compassionate as he continued. "I've long ago lost count of the tears that have been cried in this office." Once again he chuckled slightly and then said, "Did you know that your tears are precious to God?" The woman shook her head. Her tears precious? "Yes, they are." The pastor flipped some pages in his Bible that lay open to one side on his desk. "It says right here in Psalm 56:8, *'You keep track of all my sorrows. You have collected all my tears in your bottle. You have recorded each one in your book.'"*

"Why would He do that?" She was touched to the core of her being with the thought that God — or anyone — would consider her tears as something to be collected.

"Just because He loves you." The pastor spoke kindly and matter-of-fact. "Would you like to tell me what's troubling you? I would truly like to be of help, if I am able."

The woman believed this man before her. She believed he did care, and not because it was his job to do so. She somehow believed he cared because of God. People who knew God, she deduced, who sincerely knew Him, all seemed to care about other people.

"Well, I do feel silly, but what has happened to me today is very real." She took another tissue from the box and wiped her eyes.

"Would you like a glass of water?" The pastor asked, but before she could answer he had walked over to a water machine in the corner of his office by the door. He took a paper cup, held it beneath the tap and pressed a button. "Here you are," he said as he placed the cup of water on the desk next to the box of tissues.

"Thank you." The woman lifted the cup and sipped. She didn't really want it, but felt she must take notice of his kindness. One sip did actually help her scratchy throat. Probably scratchy from all the crying, she thought, as she took another welcome swallow of the cool water.

The pastor was waiting patiently, giving her the feeling that he had all the time in the world. She knew he did not; pastors were always busy taking care of people. She was thankful for his genuine kindness.

Setting down the cup and taking a deep breath, she began. "It all started when I woke up this morning." Her narrative of the day's events began slowly, interspersed with more crying. Sometimes her recounting of events was choked in sobs, but she pressed on, determined to do what she had come here to do.

When she got to the part about her sun bathing she could not get her breath. The sobs burst forth and she thought she might vomit. "I need — I need the ladies room," she managed to retch the words from her throat followed by a gagging sound.

"Certainly," the pastor was quick to action. He walked briskly to the door, called the receptionist, and was back at the woman's side in a flash. He took hold of one elbow and helped to steady her as she stood up. The woman felt another hold on her other elbow. It was the receptionist. "Come this way, my dear." Her words were soft. The woman followed, ever so grateful to be led away before she succumbed to throwing up all over the pastor's carpet.

Once they were in the ladies room, the receptionist left her. She was thankful for that as she heaved the contents of her stomach into the toilet bowl. She had only eaten a small tuna sandwich. Even so, the urge to vomit was so great that she was overpowered by repetitive dry heaves. When the heaving and gagging finally stopped, she rose, went to the sink, and splashed water on her face for several minutes. It was cold and soothing.

She patted her face dry, smoothed her hair, and opened the door. The receptionist was standing nearby, waiting, the woman supposed, for her to exit.

"Can I get you anything?" The receptionist asked with concern in her voice.

"No — I — I'm better now. Sorry about that."

"You have no need to apologize." The kind receptionist spoke as she came toward the woman, "We all get upset at times." The receptionist was holding her elbow again and leading her back to the pastor's office. His door was open, but he was not at his desk. He was looking at his shelves of books, holding one volume in his hands.

"We're back now," the receptionist said lighthearted and cheerfully, as if they had just returned from an afternoon of shopping. She led the woman back to her chair. As the woman sat down, the receptionist called out as she made her exit, "I'm nearby if you need anything."

The woman smiled her thanks to the kind receptionist and the door closed.

"I didn't see that coming," the woman began in a tone of apology. The pastor waved it off with a literal flick of his hand as he said, "You've been through a great trauma today. Your feelings are most understandable."

"Then, you believe everything I've told you?" The woman asked with a mixture of surprise and relief.

"I see no reason not to believe you," the pastor spoke while he looked into her eyes. The woman dropped her gaze to the edge of the desk. She didn't like looking into his eyes. It was like he could see into her soul; and yet, his penetrating gaze filled her with a feeling of peace and trust. Yes, she felt she could trust this man. He had — he had — well, she decided, he had 'Jesus eyes'.

What made her think that? Oh yes, the framed picture of Jesus that glowed in the dark around the edges. Her mother had given it to her when she was a little girl, afraid when the lights went out. She had liked the picture. She knew it wasn't really Jesus. No one knew what Jesus looked like, but she liked the eyes in the picture. She pretended they were real and that His ever watchful eyes were keeping her safe in the night from all unknown evil creatures that might make their way into her closet or under her bed.

She glanced up at the face of the pastor who had taken his seat behind the desk. She asked, "Do you have any idea where that envelope came from? I mean, do you think — well, I don't know about these things, but — well, the thought came to me that maybe — maybe — an angel put it there?" She looked at the pastor, her lips tight together in embarrassment. She felt her shoulders shrug up and then down as if to say, who knows? Probably not.

"I'm not an expert on angel activity," the pastor began. "I mean," I've had no personal experiences myself, but I do fully believe in angels, and that they are here on earth to watch over us, to assist us, and to protect us as God directs them to do so."

"Really?" The woman did not try to hold back the element of astonishment in her voice.

"Really," the pastor answered with a smile. "I believe it because it's what the Bible teaches. I have found that believing and obeying everything that is in the Bible has always been for my own benefit."

The pastor looked again at the Bible that lay on his desk, and he flipped some pages just as he had done earlier. "Here we are," he said, "Hebrews 13:2, *'Don't forget to show hospitality to strangers, for some who have done this have entertained angels without realizing it.'*"

"Here's another one," he said as he quickly flipped the pages. "Let's see." He flipped a few more pages. "Ah, here it is: Psalm 91, beginning with verse 9, *'If you make the Lord your refuge, if you make the Most High your shelter, no evil will conquer you; no plague will come near your home. For He will order His angels to protect you wherever you go.'"*

The pastor looked at the woman who sat before him. She looked puzzled over what he had just read. "Let me read on," he said, "and then I would like to explain something. Is that okay?"

The woman nodded her agreement so the pastor continued. "The next several verses say this: *'They will hold you up with their hands so you won't even hurt your foot on a stone. You will trample upon lions and cobras; you will crush fierce lions and serpents under your feet! The Lord says, 'I will rescue those who love me. I will protect those who trust in My name.'"*

The pastor pushed the Bible over to one side and said to the woman, "I'm not a mind reader, but I'm going to make an educated guess that at this point you may be wondering how that can be true when bad things happen to Christians — and non-Christians — all the time." He paused before asking, "Am I right?"

The woman laughed slightly and said, "That's exactly what I was wondering. Those verses that say you will trample lions and be rescued and no evil will come your way — I don't mean to be disrespectful, but it all sounds hokey to me."

The pastor laughed as he said, "There was a time it all sounded hokey to me, too." He chuckled some more. Yes, the woman thought to herself, she liked this pastor. He seemed real.

Her thoughts were interrupted as the pastor continued, "Let me see if I can explain it. First of all, the Scripture doesn't say, as you said, that no evil will come your way. It says that no evil will conquer you. Now that's a whole different picture than 'no evil will come your way.' Of course, that doesn't explain the part that says, 'you will trample upon lions and cobras.'"

The pastor shifted in his seat as he pressed on to shed more light upon the subject. "What this Scripture is implying, as all Scripture teaches, is that if you are a child of God, you needn't fear anything that may come your way."

"As an example, let's say there comes a time when a Christian follows God, perhaps to the jungle. He gets bitten by a poisonous snake but doesn't get hurt. Or," the pastor continued as he leaned forward, "let's say someone follows God to the jungle, and he gets bitten by a poisonous snake — and dies." He paused for effect before asking the rhetorical question, "If one Christian obeys God, goes to the jungle and lives through a poisonous snake bite, and another Christian also obeys God, goes to the jungle, and dies from a poisonous snake bite — have they both been saved from evil conquering them? Answer — absolutely!"

The woman was fascinated. She, too, leaned forward, her body language revealing that she didn't want to miss a word. The pastor could see that he had her full attention. In his heart he prayed, asking God to guide his words, asking the Holy Spirit to give this woman understanding.

"Would you say," the pastor was looking directly into her eyes, willing her to understand, "that God had been watching over both of them?"

The woman wrinkled her face in confusion. "I — well — one still dies. That's not protection from evil."

"Ah!" The pastor smiled triumphantly. The woman was caught in his enthusiasm; she could barely wait for his next words. "That's the whole point — neither Christian dies." The woman's face was a picture of astonishment. The pastor quickly continued lest he lose her attention, "Oh, one dies physically on earth while the other one is saved physically; but, the one who dies physically is immediately alive and with Jesus in heaven for eternity — and — another important fact of this story — both Christians would have had God's own peace and courage that would have joyfully brought them through the ordeal — whether in death or in life. So you see, as the Scripture says, "evil did not conquer them," meaning evil had no control over them or over their destiny.

The woman let out a breath of air as she sat back in her chair in amazement at the pastor's explanations. He leaned back, too, not saying anything more for the moment, giving the woman time to digest what he had just explained. The woman looked at the pastor, smiled sheepishly and said, "I'm not trying to be difficult, but just to try and get a point cleared in my mind — what if a non-Christian went to the jungle simply out of the goodness of his or her heart just wanting to help people? Suppose he or she gets bitten by this poisonous snake and lives or dies? There would have been no angels assigned to help — so..." The woman completed the unfinished sentence with the palms of her hands pointed up, her body language clearly asking, "How do you explain that one?"

"Very good point to make," the pastor spoke as if congratulating her. She did, in fact, feel exonerated from anything foolish she might have said. She smiled, and the pastor began more explanations.

"It's a matter of how we die and where we go when we meet our demise. I don't mean how we die as in, if it's by accident, disease, or old age. I mean, if we die a child of God or not."

The woman was suddenly appearing uncomfortable. The pastor hurried on without the slightest pause. He did not want to lose the woman's undivided attention.

"You see," the pastor was looking intently at the woman, "we all die, Christian or non-Christian — and — we all actually live on in eternity." The woman could not help but blink in surprise. She could even feel her eyes open wide. She felt somewhat embarrassed, but the pastor just kept explaining. "It's simple really," he said. "A Christian lives eternally with his or her Father — God — in heaven. A non-Christian lives eternally with the one he or she has chosen to follow — Satan — in hell."

The woman winced. This is what she didn't like — all this talk about hell. "Why would a loving God send anyone to such a place of torment — for eternity? Oh!" She clapped a hand over her mouth. "I didn't mean to say that out loud. It just came out!"

"It's alright," the pastor assured her, "That's another very good question." She felt embarrassed for asking, but glad, too. She never had understood how Christians, who claim that God loves everyone, can accept the fact that He sends those who don't agree with Him to hell. I mean, really! Talk about hypocrisy! Where is respect for a differing opinion? She felt herself begin to seethe. Suddenly, her thoughts were interrupted by what the pastor said next.

"Well, first of all, something that so many don't understand is this: God doesn't send anyone to hell." The woman crinkled her face into a picture of disbelief, or was it just skepticism showing?

The pastor went on. "You see, we mustn't forget that in the very beginning of time as we know it God created a perfect world for the first people that He made after His own image — Adam and Eve. There was no pain, grief, tears, or death. It was a place of perfection; a result of God's perfect love." The pastor was in his element, explaining God's plan of salvation from the beginning. The woman seemed to be devouring his every word, for which he was thankful.

"God enjoyed a perfect love relationship with the man and woman he created. He loved loving them; and, He loved them loving Him. However, God didn't want them to love Him out of His own insistence. That would be robotic, not love at all. He wanted them to love Him out of their own heart."

"I liken it to parents with their children. They could threaten and force their children to say the words 'I love you' but that wouldn't be love, would it?" The woman shook her head in agreement that, no, it would not be love. "It means so much more when anyone tells you they love you just because they really do." The pastor smiled and asked, "Don't you agree?"

"Yes, I do." The woman answered.

The seething that had started to ignite moments earlier was already replaced by a real desire to know the truth. Somehow she surprised herself by this thought; she felt she might be on the road of genuine discovery. She continued listening, straining her ears to catch every word, capturing every nuance of his explanation.

"Adam and Eve made their choice. They disobeyed God." The pastor suddenly suspended his talk. He was gazing at the ceiling as if in another world far away. "How that must have broken — no — crushed God's heart. He knew His way was perfect, and mankind would live in eternal love and joy. Equally, He knew mankind's way was imperfect, selfish, evil, and led to separation from God. There would be no love and joy to live in forever." The pastor was still staring at the ceiling.

Then — as if a spell had been broken, the pastor snapped back to attention, leaned forward and asked the woman, "Do you know why it's evil for man to choose His own way?" The woman said nothing but shook her head. She did not know why

God considered it evil for man not to choose Him. Again, she mused, that action did not sound like love to her. True love still accepts one when there is disagreement.

"It's because of God's holiness." He looked at her, indicating, she felt, that nothing more needed to be said. In fact, she was still full of confusion. She was relieved, therefore, when the pastor took up the reigns of conversation and continued on. "God has always been, is now, and always will be holy — separated out." He cannot change that about Himself. He desires close relationship with mankind that He has created, but He can only relate with holiness because He is holy all the time."

The pastor, who had taken on a somber mood, began to spring into joy, even excitement, as he spoke the next words. "That's why He made a plan that would forgive mankind for choosing to go their own way rather than to stay on the path of perfection that He designed for them. He could have washed His hands of them," he said, making a gesture of washing his hands. "Instead, he made a plan to pay the price for mankind's sinful choice. The penalty then paid, mankind could come back into loving relationship with Him because man would now be holy, too! Isn't that wonderful? God didn't have to do it, but His own love compelled Him."

The woman nodded, only slightly. Something was happening inside her that she wasn't certain she wanted to acknowledge. She was softening toward God. What? What did her mind just say to her? She must get a grip! The pastor is persuasive. Don't get trapped! Stay tuned in. He's an expert at leading one away from their own choices. But no, he wasn't leading her to any choice; he was just explaining what happened all those years ago. Oh, the battle that was taking place in her mind! Debating thoughts throwing dark spears of confusion into her heart.

No! She inwardly shouted at her thoughts. She shook herself free with grave determination to listen to this man. "I admit, I never saw it quite like that before." She heard her own voice. "I've been to Sunday School as a child." She looked up at the pastor. "You know my parents, so I guess you know they took me to church."

"What I do know about them is that they love you deeply." The woman nodded and smiled. Yes, she had to admit, she knew they loved her and wanted the best for her at all times. In fact, it seemed she couldn't do anything to make them stop loving her. Not that she would ever want them to.

The woman scooted back in her chair before saying, "Because God wanted to make a way for mankind to have relationship with Him again," she paused to sort her words, "that's why He sent Jesus? Jesus was the perfect payment for mankind's sin?"

The pastor smiled kindly with a sparkle of gladness in his eyes. "That's exactly right. Adam and Eve's choice rendered mankind unholy. A holy God simply cannot have relationship with anything opposite His holiness. It just can't be done!" The pastor's words were emphatic but warmhearted.

"I — I think I'm beginning to understand." She almost whispered as she said, "All those years in church, why didn't I see this before?" She was really speaking to herself, but the pastor answered, "Everyone has their own special time as the Holy Spirit reveals truth to each one. He knows the best time for each of us. Don't try to figure it out. Just be glad."

The pastor's smile was so infectious that the woman felt the corners of her own lips point upward. "Would you," the pastor began, his words soft, "like to ask Jesus into your life right now?"

Suddenly, as if breaking free from a time warp, the woman was hurled back to her present situation. The mysterious envelope. The message inside. A woman's right over her own life. When does life begin? Her face screwed up into a contortion of sheer torment.

"I — we," She gulped and swallowed hard. "We haven't talked about what I really came here to — to ask — to talk —"

"I have an idea. It's already late." The pastor glanced at the wall clock, "Nearly 5:30."

"Oh, I am sorry," the woman spoke in sudden embarrassment and frustration.

"No, no!" The pastor hurried to assure her. "What I am suggesting is this: my wife is out late this evening. She won't be home until 8:00pm. I'm on dinner duty," he said with amusement and chuckled. "On the menu tonight is my specialty — the only thing I know how to cook, actually." More chuckles. "Why don't you come to our house at 8:30 and join us for dinner?"

Before she could answer, the pastor continued, "If you don't mind me sharing with my wife what we have discussed thus far. My wife is a woman of great wisdom and discernment. She's my right arm in ministry. What a gift God gave in giving her to me."

The pastor walked around his desk and the woman stood, too. "I fully believe that whatever is troubling you my wife will be key in helping." He paused. The woman said nothing. "Will you come? 8:30? Spaghetti?" The woman smiled but still didn't speak. "Did I mention garlic bread and salad?"

This time the woman laughed and heard herself say, "8:30. I'll be there."

The pastor's mouth broke into a wide grin. He wrote down his home address on the back of one of his business cards and handed it to the woman. Then he walked to the door and held it open for her. The woman walked through and noticed the receptionist grabbing her purse and a sweater.

"Oh, I hope I didn't keep you working late," the woman said apologetically.

"No, not at all," the receptionist smiled. "I always leave between 5:30 and 6:00. Your timing is actually perfect." The woman was so thankful for the kindness she had been shown today.

She turned to the pastor. "Good-bye and thank you." He shook her hand. "My wife and I will see you at 8:30." Nodding her agreement, she headed for the door, hand in her purse, fishing for car keys.

Once outside, she felt the late afternoon sun kiss her face. She let out a sigh. It's been tough, so far today, she said to herself, but — I'm hopeful that I — I really am on a road of discovery. She started the engine and pulled away, heading home.

THE MESSAGE DRAWS TO A CLOSE

As the woman opened her front door, she actually felt a — a what? A peace of sorts. Yes. Strange, after all the bewilderment of the day thus far. She looked at the envelope on the coffee table and at the pages strewn on the floor where she had let them slip away. Although still troubled, she didn't feel total devastation as she thought about reading the remainder of the message.

What she did feel was a compulsion. She had to finish reading the message before 8:00pm when she would make her way to the pastor's house. I wonder what his wife is like, her thoughts took a new turn as they tried to envision this woman whom the pastor called — what was it? Oh yes, his right arm in ministry. Wow. What a compliment to one's wife. That doesn't happen much these days.

The woman went to the bathroom and splashed more cold water on her face.

She sure did a lot of water splashing today, she mused. She scrutinized the appearance of her eyes in the mirror. Yes, they were still red. Well, she told herself in surrender to her situation, I'm sure the pastor and his wife have dealt with masses of red eyes staring at them. I won't be the first or the last. She dried her face on the soft towel hanging nearby.

She walked to the kitchen, poured a small glass of apple juice, and returned to the couch and to the waiting pages on the floor. Gathering the pages together and putting them in proper order, she tucked her legs beneath her, leaned back, and began. Could she get through the last of the pages with no tears, she asked herself? Probably not, she decided. Oh well. "Let's go," her heart told her brain. Let's finish this.

"Mommy, I'm getting big now. Well, that's how I felt when Jesus told me that between weeks 20 to 23 I grew eyebrows, and tooth buds formed in my gums. The buds mean that teeth were going to sprout in my mouth like flowers pushing out of the ground. Oh, I know lots about flowers, Mommy. I learned all about them in heaven. Did you know I would have grown up to be a florist, Mommy? That's what Jesus said. I guess that's why I love all the flowers in heaven. They're so beautiful. I hope you get to see them one day. There are animals, too, in heaven, Mommy. Did you know that?"

The woman sighed. "No, I didn't know that," she said aloud. "I never thought about it; I guess I never thought about a lot of things."

"What's the name of your dog, Mommy? Sometimes I could hear him barking. I didn't know what it was, but when I asked Jesus about it, He told me it was a dog."

A dog? What could that mean? The woman thought, for the first time in today's state of affairs, here is something that doesn't make sense. I don't have a dog. Perhaps this is a hoax after all.

She drained her glass of apple juice with one long swallow and took the empty glass back to the kitchen. She was placing it in the sink and looking out the window at her backyard when she heard it. She drew in a sharp breath. She pulled open the sliding glass door and stepped outside, her ears acutely tuned in to her neighbor's dog — barking!

She jumped back inside, slid the door shut, and nearly ran to the pages waiting for her. Picking them up, she scanned the words to come back to the last sentence she had read about the dog. The narrative continued. "You'll like all the animals in heaven, Mommy, and guess what? They're all friendly to each other! There's no fighting in heaven."

No fighting in heaven. The woman pondered this for a moment. How lovely that would be. If animals don't fight, I'm sure humans don't either. Funny, I've always known about heaven but, well, I never considered it to be a real place. The woman was somewhat startled by this admission to herself. I must read on, she admonished herself, as much to let go of the thoughts about heaven as to simply come to the end of the message before 8:00pm.

"When I was 24 weeks old, guess what was happening to me? My lungs were getting formed. They were going to help me breathe when I left my tummy house. I wasn't supposed to leave my tummy house until I was nine months old. I was getting ready, Mommy. It was almost time, but then something happened when I was six months old. It was awful then, Mommy, but I can talk about it now. In heaven all the pain and tears we had on earth are taken away. Jesus put His own happiness in my heart as soon as I got here. We all get His happiness when we get to heaven. Did you know that, Mommy?"

"No," the woman said again, "I didn't know that." Fresh tears were forming. She plucked several tissues from a nearby box ready for what she knew would be the hardest part of reading this message.

"I remember one day a bright light was hurting my eyes. Were you taking a sunbath again, Mommy? It's okay. I just turned over, but then something scary happened. Mommy, something I never felt before came into my tummy house. I didn't know what it was, and I tried to get away. I was pushing with my feet. *Mommy, did you feel me?* I was moving my arms to twirl around and get away, but I couldn't, Mommy. It got me. I'm sorry, Mommy. I tried to stay with you, but this awful thing got my legs and pulled and pulled and — Mommy it hurt so bad! I opened my mouth to scream, but no one could hear me. Then — it was all over."

The woman opened her own mouth to scream but nothing came out. What a picture of torment — mouth open, tears gushing, face flushed red, hands grabbing fistfuls of hair. She threw herself to her knees on the floor, her face burrowing itself into the carpet. "Oh, God!" She found her voice and wailed in agony, "I didn't know! Dear God, I didn't know!"

She coughed. She gagged. Her stomach, tied in knots of despair, responded with multiple, retching, dry heaves. For a moment she thought she would faint and wished that she would. Faint! Pass out! She willed herself into another world, a world where reality would vanish and she could once again walk the path of never having known.

She coughed, nearly vomiting again. Then, taking long, slow, deep breaths, her body began to gain some control. When she knew the heaving had stopped, she let her feeble body fall onto its side like a rag tossed away, limp and feeling absolutely useless.

She was frozen in emotional exhaustion, able only to blink her eyes once in a while. She stared at the individual carpet fibers. One fiber caught her attention. There was no reason — she just stared, having no motivation or strength to move a muscle.

Suddenly, her body shot bolt upright. What time is it? Panic was trying to make her stomach go into dry heave mode again. No! Breathe deep and slow. She obeyed her silent command, moving to her knees, and then brought her body to a sitting position on the couch.

Oh, good. Just a few minutes past 7:00pm. There was still time. She had to do this. She had to finish reading the words that both tormented and compelled her to go on.

"I like being in heaven, Mommy. I wanted to stay with you so much, and I hope you're not too sad that I left you. It wasn't my choice, Mommy. I would have stayed. I would have been a florist. I would have done lots of things, but don't worry, Mommy. It's beautiful here in heaven."

The woman lay the pages on her lap to continue reading as her hands were trembling. "Mommy, Jesus says that anyone can come to heaven, but He doesn't *make* anyone come. Every person has to decide if they want to come. Do you want to come, Mommy? I hope so. I asked Jesus how you could get here. Do you know what He said, Mommy? He said for you to just tell Him you accept His gift of life forever, and tell Him you're sorry for wrong things you've done. Jesus said that everybody has done wrong things, but guess what, Mommy? Jesus said no matter how bad someone has been, He will forgive them of anything at all, and He will throw the bad away. Isn't that amazing, Mommy?"

"Yes, that's amazing. But it's hard to believe." The woman spoke out loud, looking at the pages, as if somehow the words itself could hear her.

"I know it's hard to believe, Mommy." The woman gasped, then read on. "Sometimes people come here and say they were so bad on earth they can hardly believe Jesus really forgave them, but they know it's true. You know how they can tell, Mommy? Remember, I told you — Jesus gives everyone who comes here His own happiness. His happiness lasts forever."

The woman managed to let a slight smile form at the corners of her mouth. "Happiness forever — that would indeed be heavenly. But I don't deserve it."

The woman talked out loud for several minutes, arguing with herself, with the words on the paper, with the very idea of forgiveness forever. Could it be so? When the last of any argument had vacated her thoughts, she turned her eyes one last time to the pages.

"I have to go now, Mommy. I'm so glad that Jesus let me write to you. I wanted you to know that I'm happy here, but that I would have never left you on purpose. I tried to stay in my tummy house, Mommy. I can't come back to you now, but Mommy, one day, will you come to me? I love you, Mommy. Jesus said to tell you that He loves you, too. He always has and He always will."

The woman seemed to have no more thoughts to think. She gently folded the pages and put them back into the white envelope. She took it with her to her bedroom and lay it back on the bedside table where she had found it that morning.

In zombie fashion, she splashed more cold water onto her face and applied makeup to try to cover the results of the day's anguish. Changing her clothes, she took one last look into the mirror, decided no more could be done, picked up her purse, and left the house.

She arrived promptly at 8:30pm. How she managed the punctual arrival was rather astonishing, considering her state of mind in the last hour. She was relieved that she had not been late.

As she rang the doorbell, a flush of nervousness washed over her. She tried to swallow, but her mouth was dry. Why did I come? Run away! No! I may find help. You don't deserve help! The door opened.

"Come in," a pleasant, smiling face greeted her. "My husband has told me all about you. I'm so glad you've come."

The woman stepped inside, smelling the delicious aroma of sautéed onions that filled the air. Her mouth watered. Good, she could swallow away the feeling of cotton in her throat. She took a deep breath, smiled at the lady in return, and followed her to the dining room.

She thought again of being on a road of discovery. Perhaps there really is something — something about God — that she can discover and that will make a difference to her life. She surprised herself by sincerely hoping so.

THE PRO-LIFE DISCUSSION

"Ta-da!" The jovial pastor placed a large bowl of spaghetti at the center of the table. The thin, white pasta was covered with a most tempting tomato sauce, thick with chunks of tomatoes, beef, peppers, onions, and garlic. A delicious, crisp looking salad and a little wicker basket of garlic bread graced each side of the spaghetti dish.

"Dinner is now served," he said in an exaggerated British accent. "May I have the honor of seating such lovely ladies?" He swept his arm in an oversized gesture to his guest and pulled out a chair for her to sit in. He repeated the gesture to his wife, helped her in her chair, and kissed her on the cheek.

Taking a seat himself, he chuckled and said, "Okay, formalities over. Let's eat." The ladies chuckled, too, and the woman was glad for the relaxed and jovial atmosphere. She already felt much better. The butterflies that had been swarming in her stomach had all calmed down from their flight.

"Shall we pray?" She heard the pastor say. Instinctively she bowed her head as the pastor told God thank you for the food and for all His blessings.

Each one helped themselves to the food before them. The woman was glad that the conversation was not immediately about her or why she had come. The pastor's wife shared her day, talking about particular events that had taken place, people she had met, plans for other days.

The pastor then talked about his day, telling of a good book he had just begun to read about the last days and the second coming of Christ. The woman didn't actually understand what he was talking about, but she smiled and nodded her head in response as if she did. He then told a joke that one of his deacons had told him.

To this the woman replied, "I wonder if telling jokes is a Biblical requirement for being a deacon. I grew up with my deacon father coming home after every meeting ready to tell us yet another new joke." She surprised herself at her own ability to be humorous at a time like this, when her day had been filled with constant inner turmoil. The pastor and his wife both laughed with her. The woman was glad she came, if for no other reason at this moment than for a much needed emotional break.

When they had all finished eating, the pastor stood to clear the table. The ladies also started to stand but were quickly reprimanded. "I'll not have that ladies. It is my pleasure to serve you both." He spoke the second sentence with his exaggerated British accent again. He took the spaghetti and returned for the salad and bread. Next he took away the plates. The ladies did not engage in much conversation during this activity. It seemed much more amusing to simply watch him and his butler act.

The woman had never considered that a pastor could be funny. Why would I think that? she mused. I suppose I only ever saw them standing behind a pulpit, preaching. She glanced at the pastor's wife who sat smiling at her husband. Her eyes were kind. Yes, the woman thought to herself. I have a feeling the pastor is right. I bet this woman really is his right arm in ministry.

The pastor had returned and asked, "Are we ready for dessert, or would we like to wait a while?"

"Oh," the woman began, "I think I need to wait."

"Definitely!" The pastor's wife agreed and added, "Let's make ourselves more comfortable in the living room."

She stood as the pastor spoke again and asked, "What about coffee for now, then?" The two women looked at each other and simultaneously nodded their heads.

"Wonderful. Milk and sugar?" He asked the woman.

"I take it black," she answered.

"Coming right up. You two go into the living room and I'll bring the coffee in."

The living room was bright with a cream colored couch and matching chairs with red and grey cushions strewn about. A vase of yellow roses was atop a bookshelf that stood against one of the walls.

"Oh, what beautiful roses!" the woman exclaimed and added, "I love roses!"

Smiling, the pastor's wife said, "Sit wherever you like." The woman chose an armchair and the pastor's wife sat in the middle of the couch. A few minutes later, when the pastor came with the coffee, he set down the mugs, one on a little table next to the woman's chair and the other two on the coffee table in front of the couch. He sat next to his wife, picked up his mug and took a sip.

Suddenly the woman felt a stab of alarm which woke up the butterflies. They were flying around her stomach again. Now was the time. The talk would soon begin; the reasons of her visit would be discussed. Did she really want this after all? Yes! No! Oh, that other voice, always contradicting her! Make an excuse to leave. No! I want help. From the church?

Her private argument with herself came to a sudden halt as she heard the pastor say, "I've shared with my wife our conversation today."

Brought back to the reality of the moment, the woman smiled weakly and suddenly felt embarrassed. The pastor's wife must have sensed the sudden change in demeanor because she said, so kindly, "Please try not to feel awkward in any way. We are both so glad that you have come. We like helping people, honestly."

The woman felt her body relax again. Yes, this was going to be okay. It might be uncomfortable, with more tears to follow, but it would be okay. She smiled her thanks to the pastor's wife and then said, "I guess your husband told you that the main reason for my coming to see him never actually got talked about."

"Yes, he did. I told him it was a wonderful idea to invite you to come tonight." Leaning forward she whispered conspiratorially, "My husband comes up with good ideas once in a while. I think I've trained him well." She looked at her husband who smiled at her joke and replied in mock exaggeration, "Yes, it's a task you've handled well, my dear."

The woman really liked this couple. What a surprise to feel comfortable and relaxed with a pastor and his wife.

She smiled with her thoughts and then said, "I'm glad we talked about the possibility of angels today. Oh, I mean the reality. Oh, dear." Embarrassment filled her senses. What a fine start! Her first words out of her mouth were words of doubt. Oh, she did hope the pastor would not be offended because it sounded as if she doubted his explanations about angels. She quickly added, "I wasn't saying I haven't believed what you told me about angels!"

"My dear," the pastor's wife was speaking, "when we're upset by anything, our words have a way of coming out all jumbled up. We say things we didn't mean to say, or we say things we're not sure we mean."

The woman smiled and said, "Thank you. I can already tell that you are a very understanding person. You are both understanding — and compassionate."

"We're glad you feel so," the pastor's wife responded, and then added, tenderly but directly, "My dear, it's not really angels that you want to discuss again, is it?"

The woman dropped her gaze to the floor and answered, "No. I want to talk about something entirely different."

The pastor's wife smiled and said nothing more. Several seconds passed or was it an eternity? The woman suddenly couldn't get words to come out of her mouth. Her mind could not make out what to say. She fidgeted.

The pastor spoke this time, "I find when I'm troubled, and I know I need to speak to someone, and the words don't want to come out —"

The woman lifted her head to look directly at him. She wanted to hear his words of advice. She so wanted to tell them about the Message; by the same token, she did not.

"I just close my eyes and blurt it out." The pastor sort of shrugged his shoulders as if to imply that he knew that idea might not work for her but was it worth a try?

The woman smiled and shrugged her shoulders, too. Then she closed her eyes. Actually, she did feel a bit calmer with her eyes shut. Just say it, she willed her mouth to form words. "I aborted my baby!" She squeezed her eyes tight, not wanting to open them again, but she did open them, and she did look up at the pastor and his wife.

"We thought that to be the case," the pastor's wife smiled with a tenderness in her eyes as she said further, "and it troubles you so, you poor dear."

The woman could hardly believe what she was hearing. They weren't surprised at her announcement? They were sorry for her torment? They still showed her kindness even though what she had done was against what they believed? "How — how did you know? I mean, what made you think it was — was that?" Feeling ashamed, the woman lowered her head and stared at her mug of coffee as she listened to the reply.

It was the pastor who spoke. "As I was praying for you on my way home tonight, after we talked, it came to my mind that the real trouble was — abortion."

"It was the same with me." This time it was the pastor's wife who was talking as she explained, "When my husband phoned to tell me you were coming and briefly told me some of the conversation you shared together, it came to me, too, that the real matter was abortion."

The woman looked up then, her face a picture of grief and shame, a painting of misery and remorse framed in sheer confusion. "I don't know how you could have known."

"My dear," the pastor's wife said simply, "it's the Holy Spirit who reveals such things. He tells us things we could not know without His own revelation. It keeps us looking to Him and reminds us always that living in the power of the Holy Spirit is the only way to live in peace and harmony with ourselves." Her smile broadened as she added, "It's the only way anyone can effectively help someone else." Then she added, "We want to help you, dear."

With this the woman's face crumpled. The pastor was quick to deliver a box of tissues to the little table beside her. She plucked a few and held them to her nose as if in doing so the tears would not come after all. But they did come, slowly at first and then in full stream. She made no noise; she just cried. When at last there were no more tears to flow, she wiped her eyes, blew her nose, and looked up sheepishly.

"When did it happen, dear?" The pastor's wife asked.

"Four months ago." The woman met the gaze of the pastor's wife, then lowered her eyes to the floor.

"Were you confused at the time?"

"No. No, I was certain. Everything was certain. It seemed the right thing for me; my right to choose for my own body." She lifted her face then and asked, "Every woman, every person, has a right to choose what to do with their own body — don't they?"

"Of course," the pastor's wife said, "everyone has a right to choose for their own body — but no one has the right to choose for someone else's body."

The woman's brow crinkled into lines of deep thought. She knew what the pastor's wife was saying. She understood that, in aborting, she had made a choice for her baby; she had made a choice for someone else's body. It all seemed clear now, but wait! No! It's a fetus! It's not a life — is it?

"Did you know that at six weeks of age the heart begins to beat in the fetus?" The woman heard the words come out of her mouth. She asked the question, but not because she thought they didn't know. She was saying out loud, finally, what had triggered her trip on this present road of emotional turmoil.

"Did you know that four months ago?" The pastor's wife asked, her voice still tender, her face a picture of sincere care for the troubled woman before her.

"No. No, I didn't know. They told me that a fetus isn't a life. They said we're not killing babies; we're getting rid of a fetus that would turn into a baby, but it wasn't yet a baby. We were getting rid of something that wasn't convenient for me at the time. It was my right; it was my right to choose." She paused, as more tears came. "That's what they told me."

The woman dabbed at her eyes again and explained, "This morning, when I read in the letter that the heart beats at six weeks — it — it hit me then — if there is no life, how can a heart beat? I mean, we say a person is dead when the heart stops beating. So — it came to me — if a life is dead when a heart stops beating, then a life has to be living when a heart is beating." She looked up. "Isn't that just — well — common sense?"

It was the pastor who spoke next. "Yes, a beating heart is certainly a sign of life. Non-living things don't have beating hearts. But, did you know," he said in earnest, "life begins, not when the heart beats, but at conception, when the sperm and the egg connect?" She shook her head. The pastor continued, "The beating heart at six weeks is just a sign to us that the life that began at conception is indeed developing. It's like the first audible sound that says triumphantly, 'I'm still here!'"

The woman was looking fully at both the pastor and his wife when she asked, "How do you know? How do you know that life begins at conception?"

"Ah!" sounded the pastor as he stood and walked over to the bookshelf. He removed a Bible, opened it and read, "'*You made all the delicate, inner parts of my body and knit me together in my mother's womb. Thank you for making me so wonderfully complex! Your workmanship is marvelous — and how well I know it. You watched me as I was being formed in utter seclusion, as I was woven together in the dark of the womb. You saw me before I was born. Every day of my life was recorded in your book. Every moment was laid out before a single day had passed.'* This is from Psalm 139," the pastor said. "Isn't it interesting that the

Scripture says, 'You saw me before I was born?' How can God see a *me* if what has formed is lifeless?"

The woman assumed the pastor was asking the question rhetorically, not expecting an answer. He was gazing at the ceiling for a moment as if collecting his thoughts together. He then asked, "Is a cell alive?"

"Pardon?" The woman asked. She had heard the question but didn't quite understand it.

"Is a cell alive?" The pastor repeated the question. He was looking directly at the woman, his gaze steady, unmoving. The woman felt uncomfortable. Was she supposed to know the answer to this question? It's not like I'm a scientist, she retorted in the privacy of her mind.

At this point, his wife jumped back into the conversation. "For some people, it's hard to believe what the Bible teaches; it's much easier to believe what science is said to have discovered." The pastor's wife had walked over to the same book shelf where her husband had stood moments before. She pulled a book off the shelf and returned to her place on the couch. "Would you agree with that statement?" She was looking at the woman, smiling, waiting for her answer.

"Well, yes, I suppose it's easier to believe something that has been tested and proved. Science does that — proves things. The Bible just — says things." Feeling more awkward, she hurried on with, "Oh, I am sorry. That was rude in regard to what you believe. I am sorry."

"No need for apology, my dear," the pastor's wife spoke genuinely. "You are in the majority with that line of thinking." She then began to flip through the pages of the book, clearly looking for something specific.

Her husband looked on, nodding his head in agreement. The woman surmised that he obviously knew what his wife was looking for. They were a good team. One seemed to know what the other was about to say before they said it. Well, the woman deduced, they've been doing this a long time.

When the pastor's wife had found her place, she lay the book open on her lap and said, "This is a medical book. It was compiled by scientists and medical doctors. It's a book that deals specifically with pregnancy. You may know this already, but I hope to make a helpful point," she explained.

"Oh yes," said the woman with a note of enthusiasm in her voice. "If some scientific medical explanation will be helpful to my mixed-up brain right now, I will be most grateful." She even managed a smile, which was returned by the pastor's wife as she pointed to the open pages on her lap and said, "It explains here that after the sperm finds the egg and merges with it, it takes on the name of zygote."

The pastor's wife held the book closer to her face at this point and read, "A zygote is the joining of an egg and the sperm in order to create a new organism. In other words, a zygote is the fertilized egg. In 24 hours, the zygote divides itself into two cells. This procedure of dividing takes place with every new cell created, every

12 hours. These cells form all the parts of the body."

The pastor sort of chuckled, as he declared with an element of awe in his voice, "Every cell in our body creates more cells. Who, but an awesome creator God, could have done such a thing?"

The woman didn't answer, supposing the pastor to be asking rhetorically again. Even so, she found something inside herself feel...what? A sort of excitement. Yes, she thought, as a matter of fact, she did feel rather excited at the wonder of this cell creation. Her attention was suddenly drawn away from her private thoughts as the pastor's wife began to speak again.

"This is a medically proven, scientific fact — the dividing of these cells to create even more cells. Also," the pastor's wife was reading from the book again, "at the nucleus of every cell in the human body there is located a set of 23 chromosomes. These chromosomes record the genetic makeup of the body."

This time it was the pastor's wife who let out a slight chuckle as she declared, "Even if I weren't a Christian, God creating these things seems much easier to believe as opposed to the 'big bang theory' that wants us to believe that the tiniest of cells came about randomly because of an explosion. What do you think, dear? Is it easier to believe that God created life or that an explosion created life?"

The woman blinked and then, to everyone's surprise, she laughed as she said, "Well, put like that, an explosion forming life does seem a bit — way out there!" She laughed again. Both the pastor and his wife smiled as they glanced at each other. It was good to see this troubled young woman have a moment of laughter, and if the laughter was the result of seeing some truth — all the better.

The woman chuckled a bit more, the pastor and his wife joining in; then all sounds of hilarity faded into silence. The woman was rubbing her hands together. She seemed to be contemplating or perhaps forming in her mind a new question to ask. Neither the pastor nor his wife spoke; they waited instead for the woman to speak when she was ready.

"Do you know what I was thinking as I drove over here?" She looked at them both and then lowered her gaze to study the carpet.

"No," the pastor answered, "what were you thinking as you drove over here?"

"This thought about Mars suddenly jumped into my head."

"Mars?" The pastor asked.

"The planet Mars?" The pastor's wife wanted to clarify.

"Yes," the woman answered, as she lifted her gaze from the carpet to their interested faces, "the planet Mars. You talking about cells has reminded me of it." She hurriedly went on to explain. "You see, I watched a program on TV a few weeks ago. It was about NASA and the hopes of finding signs of life on Mars." The woman paused here to collect her thoughts together and then continued,

"The scientists seem to get very excited at the thought of finding just one molecule or bacteria or some other cellular type of organism."

The woman's brow crinkled, deep lines forming. She rubbed her forehead, trying to form her next words. Then she looked at the pastor and his wife and asked, "If science hopes to discover one particle of water or one cell of anything with belief that it proves life, then why, with cells forming from the moment of conception in a woman's body, do they say those cells are not yet life?"

Both the pastor and his wife smiled as the wife said, "I think you're on a path of discovery, my dear."

"Yes," the woman agreed, but not with a smile. A very troubled look etched itself all over her face. "If this is right — if a cell is a living thing which proves life, then..." The woman clasped her hands over her mouth and bent forward in anguish. She couldn't breathe!

She felt something on her shoulder. She opened her eyes and glanced up to see the hand of the pastor's wife. The woman lifted her tear soaked face, and the pastor's wife sat on the arm of the chair and cradled the woman's head in her arms. She stroked her hair, whispering comforting words.

The woman knew she had to speak out the words — those horrible words! No! Go home now! You're not the only woman who has made this choice. Oh, these voices in my head! It's not the end of the world, her reason told her. Yes, she argued with herself; but I made the choice, and it was the wrong choice! I didn't have the right! She choked here, and the pastor's wife, still cradling her head, rocked gently back and forth.

Grabbing hold of all her resolve, she pulled her body up and choked out the words, "I'm a murderer!" Sobs of anguish shook her whole body, while nausea brought wrenching noises to her mouth. She stood up, wild-eyed!

"Down the hall, first on the right," she heard the pastor's wife say. She ran, her hands clasped over her mouth, hoping with all her being that she would not vomit all over the carpet.

She lunged into the bathroom, closed the door with a bang, and knelt before the toilet. Retching noises sounded from her throat. Finally, after several minutes, she eased back and sat on the floor. Her breathing was easing, too. When she had strength to stand, she went to the sink and splashed cold water onto her face over and over again. She dried her face on a towel, looked in the mirror, and nearly began the crying and heaving process all over again. No! Get a grip!

She took a breath, held it, and let it out slowly. She waited several more minutes, both to make certain her body would not want to repeat the act before the toilet, and to gain some resolve to go out and face the pastor and his wife. What must they think? Would they want her out of their house? No, she had already told them she aborted and they showed her nothing but immense kindness. I don't deserve kindness! She scowled at herself in the mirror, loathing who she saw there. More minutes had passed. She couldn't stay in the bathroom all night. Just go!

Go now! She opened the door and to her relief, no one was there. She pictured the pastor's wife, in kindness and concern, waiting for her, but no one was there. Thank goodness!

Quietly, she made her way down the hall and back into the living room. The pastor and his wife were still there, but their heads were bent over something. Oh! Their heads were bowed. They were praying. For her? She didn't deserve prayer. She didn't deserve anything good and kind.

She wanted to make an exit then, to slip out of the house unnoticed, but that would be rude. She might not deserve kindness, but this pastor and his wife certainly did. She stayed where she was until both their heads lifted. The pastor's wife noticed her first.

"My dear!" Just those two words held a depth of genuine care. The pastor's wife stood to go to her, but the woman walked over to her chair and sat down. "I've put a glass of water there for you, dear." The pastor's wife indicated the glass. In response, the woman took a welcome sip, then another, longer drink.

She wondered what she would say, but she needn't have. The pastor took charge of the conversation. She was thankful as she listened with a grateful heart.

"My wife and I have been praying for you," he began. The woman nodded. She had seen them. She knew they were praying for her, but didn't they understand she didn't deserve prayer?

"I want to say something to you, and I want you to listen to the end. Will you do that?"

She didn't want to listen to the end. Was he going to tell her what an awful person she was? She already knew that! She wanted to get up now and leave, but she felt her head nod yes. She would stay and listen. If he wanted to berate her for being a murderer, it was no less than she deserved.

"Did you know," the pastor began, "that God is obsessed with His love for you?"

She blinked in great surprise! Even now? Even after she confessed what she had done, he was going to tell her that God loved her?

"The Bible tells us that God knows the number of hairs on your head. So when you brush your hair, and a number of hairs come out in the brush, God knows how many are still left on your head." He paused before adding with a smile, "Now, I call that obsession."

She was not ready to return his smile, but she kept listening. It was the only polite thing she could do. He deserved to be listened to.

"God had it in His plan from the beginning of time as we know it, to make a way for mankind to live with Him, in perfect joy and peace forever." The woman before him sat motionless. Was she understanding? He and his wife had prayed that the Holy Spirit would give her understanding.

He went on, "It all started in the Garden of Eden. Remember, I talked about them today when you came to my office." The woman nodded. The pastor continued, "I'd like to touch on them again. Understanding what happened in the very beginning is so helpful to understanding the heart of God."

The woman was rather amazed. Is it really possible to understand the heart of God? Does He really love, even her, obsessively? Her eyes were fastened on the pastor, absorbing his every word, craving with her last ounce of hope, that something would lead her out of the dark tunnel she had lived in for so long.

At this moment there was a battle taking place in the heavens. Angels and demons were interlocked in a mighty spiritual warfare for the very life of this woman. The pastor's wife was engaged on the frontline; she was wielding a weapon that enraged the demons — she was praying.

The pastor was continuing on without hesitation, speaking out words as the Holy Spirit brought them to his mind. "When God created Adam and Eve, He enjoyed a perfect love relationship with them. He wanted this relationship to go on forever, but —" the pastor paused to emphasize his next point, "God didn't want them to be like robots, going through the motions of walking in the ways of God. He wanted them to have free choice. You probably remember from your Sunday School days what happened."

The woman nodded. Yes, she knew the story, but somehow she felt she was about to hear something new. Suddenly, she wanted to listen. Her eyes were glued to the pastor attentively. She surprised herself with her unexpected longing to listen to all he had to say.

"Adam and Eve made their choice, but their choice was to disobey God. From that moment, God could have wiped His hands and said, 'That's it then. You have made your choice. I leave you to the destruction of your sin.' But you see," the pastor had moved to the very edge of the couch, "God just couldn't do it. He couldn't leave them to be doomed forever. He had to make a way for them. By the way," he changed tracks here for just a moment, "do you know why God wants mankind to follow His way and no other way?"

The woman shook her head. She had always supposed God was a — well, she really shouldn't feel this way she knew, but — she had always assumed God to be a control freak. He set up impossible standards just to watch people fail so He could punish them. What was the pastor going to say? She wanted to know. Her eyes remained fixed on him, her ears open to his every word.

The pastor's wife could sense the genuine interest. In her heart, she bowed herself before God. In the silence, she continued to pray that the Holy Spirit would keep the woman's ears open to truth and closed to all lies of the enemy. After all, Satan was not pleased with what was being revealed to this woman.

The pastor was now explaining, "God desires that mankind follow His way because — His way is perfection! You see, it only stands to reason that, if God is holy, perfect in love, perfect in everything, then if we follow His way, we are also on a path to obtain perfection. When we get to heaven, there will be perfect love, perfect joy, and perfect peace. Who wouldn't want that if they could have it?"

Well, that makes sense, the woman thought to herself. Yes, this is beginning to make sense. She leaned forward, her interest piqued.

"Through Adam and Eve, sin entered the world. Mankind is cursed; all of creation is cursed. However, in His obsessive love for you and for me — for all of us, God made a way to save us from this curse."

The pastor scooted back a bit here. He was studying the ceiling briefly and then told a story of sorts. He gave an illustration.

"Suppose that you committed a crime," the pastor said. "Suppose that you were arrested and brought to trial. There was no doubt that you were guilty. There was indisputable evidence of your guilt. The judge asks you to stand to accept your punishment. The judge is just about to pronounce your sentence when suddenly, the proceedings are interrupted. Someone calls to the judge to please wait. They step forward and say, 'Judge, please don't sentence this woman. Please let me take the punishment for her!' The judge answers, 'But you're not guilty of any crime; this woman is guilty.' The man is unmoved and begs the judge to give you a full pardon while he serves your sentence. The judge agrees. You are told you may go. The innocent man is taken away by the guards to pay for the crime you committed."

The woman understood what the pastor was about to say. She sensed that the innocent man in the story was Jesus. Her thoughts were confirmed when the pastor said, "That story really happened for me, my wife, for you. The innocent man is Jesus."

The woman nodded her agreement, letting the pastor know that she understood what he was saying. The pastor's wife continued on silently in joyful and earnest prayer. She perceived that the woman was open, truly considering what was being explained to her.

"The Bible tells us that the only payment for sin was a blood sacrifice. In the Old

Testament, mankind would take animals to be sacrificed for their sins. This was just a picture of the ultimate and perfect sacrifice that was yet to come — God's own Son — Jesus."

The woman nodded, suddenly feeling an awesome gratitude come over her for what Jesus had done.

"When Adam and Eve chose to sin," the pastor continued, "when they chose to disobey God, to go their own way, God Himself arranged the first blood sacrifice."

She opened her eyes in wide surprise. The pastor took note and emphasized, "Yes. The Bible tells us in Genesis 3:21 that God made clothing from animal skins for Adam and Eve. Innocent animals that Adam himself had named. Imagine how he must have felt when he realized that his sin caused an innocent animal to be killed on his behalf."

The pastor paused here, perhaps, the woman surmised, to try to imagine how Adam had felt. *She* was imagining how Adam felt. Awful! He had given names to these innocent animals and they had to be sacrificed to pay for something they didn't do. Her heart was filled with compassion for these animals. Her understanding was growing. She was beginning to sense that, yes, God was and is a God of love.

"Jesus was innocent, too," she heard the pastor say. "He was the ultimate, perfect sacrifice. You and I are the guilty ones. Jesus was innocent just like the animals who were killed for Adam and Eve. Jesus was killed, too."

The pastor let this statement linger in the air before adding, now with a smile of triumph, "But Jesus defeated death! No animal nor any other living being could defeat death, but Jesus did. He rose again on the third day and lives in heaven now, ready to make intercession for us." He looked intently at the woman and asked, "Do you know what it means that Jesus is making intercession for us?"

The woman shook her head. No, she didn't quite understand that one. She wasn't even sure what the word meant. She was anxious to know; suddenly, she was eager to know about the love of God in a manner she had never cared to know before, even in her Sunday school days.

She had enjoyed Sunday school days. She liked the stories of the Bible characters back then. What happened to her? She turned this question over in her mind. When she left her parent's home, she left their God behind, too. Life just happened, and she had chosen a path without God on it. She knew it. Her life thus far had proved what a mistake that choice had been. She felt ashamed and didn't want to think about it anymore. It disturbed her, and she was already upset since the arrival of that letter. Was it really a letter from heaven?

Abruptly, her attention returned to the present as she heard the pastor's wife calling to her, "My dear? My dear?"

"Oh!" She looked up. "I — I'm sorry. I was ..." She looked at the pastor and said, "I'm so sorry. I didn't mean to be rude. I was listening to you, really. In fact, it's the things you've been saying that sent my mind wandering." She looked sheepish, but as always, both the pastor and his wife assured her there was no need for apology.

"I believe you were explaining intercession," the woman said. "Would you mind telling me again? I do want to know what it all means."

The pastor smiled, assuring her that it would be a pleasure to explain again. "Intercession means to intervene on behalf of another. In our case, it means that Jesus intervenes on behalf of those who belong to Him. He represents His own before God the Father."

The woman wrinkled her brow trying to imagine it all; trying to understand.

The pastor continued, "You see, when someone realizes that they are doomed without Christ; when they realize why He died on the cross for them; when they then ask His forgiveness, receiving the promise of eternal life with Him; then Jesus intercedes as He stands before Father God and declares, 'This one is mine! They have been made clean by my blood; they are clothed in righteousness.' That's what intercession means."

The woman felt so drawn to all she was hearing. Like never before, she wanted to be made clean, like the pastor had just explained, but she didn't deserve such promise of eternal life where everything was joy and peace forever. No, she didn't deserve that; she could not dare ask for forgiveness for things she had done. There were too many things, anyway.

"Do you understand, dear? Any questions?" The pastor's wife was speaking, her eyes gentle, filled, it seemed to the woman, with — with — a sort of holy concern. Then it dawned on her; the pastor's wife has Jesus eyes, too, just like her husband! Strange, why should they care for her? I know it's their job, but still, why care about me?

Silence lingered. The woman guessed they were waiting for her to say something, but what could she say? Did she want what Jesus had to offer her? Yes. Did she deserve it? No! Should she say that out loud? Why not? They already know how awful I am. I might as well just confirm what we all know.

"I do understand," the woman began, "at least, I think I do." She paused to consider how much she did, in fact, understand and then added, "If I understand correctly, Jesus, the innocent one, died for the guilty ones so the guilty could be made clean."

"That's exactly right!" the pastor exclaimed rather jubilantly before continuing. "When someone receives what Jesus did for them, then the Bible tells us in Romans 5:1, '*Therefore, having been justified by faith, we have peace with God through our Lord Jesus Christ.*' Justified is like saying, just as if I'd never sinned."

The woman was touched very deeply in her heart. Could this be so? Could she be made clean by Jesus, just as if she had never sinned? But no, she dare not ask for such a thing. She did not deserve it. No! She should not ask for it! Best to just go home now. I've taken enough of their time. Yes, I'll go home. But what then? Am I doomed to misery?

"I know you are devastated about the abortion. If you've come to understand when life begins, then you will now feel immeasurably shattered." The pastor's wife was speaking with that continued gentleness in her voice. Why aren't they hating me, the woman wanted to know. She hated herself.

She heard herself say, rather robotically, "If life is in the cells, then yes, I have no choice but to believe a fetus is a baby — developing and growing everyday — it's a baby, alright. It's a baby."

Suddenly, taking a new track, the woman asked, "It seems so easy when I'm with you to believe that the fetus is alive — a developing baby. So why can't those who are pro-choice see it, too? They know cells are alive — don't they? Oh, it's all so confusing. Right now, at this moment, I'm convinced you are right, but tomorrow if I were to go back to the Planned Parenthood offices, I would probably be convinced by them all over again that the fetus isn't alive after all!" She stood then, her back and shoulders straight, her chin lifted. "I'm sorry," she said assertively, "I thank you for your time, but I'm going now. I see nothing more to be said. Thank you, again."

The pastor and his wife stood also, glancing at each other with looks of anxiety painted all over their faces. "Please don't go." It was the pastor's wife who stepped forward as she said further, "It seems you've come to no real conclusion and yet —," she paused, searching for the right words, "and yet, I feel you're standing at the crossroads, uncertain which path to take, feeling pulled in different directions all at the same time. Am I right?"

The woman nodded her head and answered, "Yes, that describes what I feel right now very well, but —" she hesitated. She had taken so much of their time already. Maybe she would never fully understand. Maybe she didn't deserve to ever understand.

It was the pastor who spoke next when he said, "I have something —" he hesitated, too, glancing at the ceiling again. It was as if all the words he ever needed were written on the ceiling. He found his words and continued, "I have something I haven't mentioned thus far. It's a video. It would be difficult to watch, probably very painful. What do you think?" He was asking his wife who replied after a thoughtful pause, "Yes, it would be painful." Then, looking at the woman she added, "But I don't think it could add any more pain than what this dear woman is going through already."

The woman felt uneasy, almost scared, and yet drawn by sheer curiosity to what they were talking about. What video? What would it show? They must feel strongly that it might help her. They wouldn't even mention it otherwise. What should she say?

"You're right," she heard her own voice, "at this point I don't think anything could make me feel any worse. If you feel this video might help, then —" she took a deep breath and let it out saying, "I'll watch it."

"Follow me," was all the pastor said as he began to exit the room. His wife indicated for the two of them to follow. Down the hall toward the back of the house they came to a den. One wall was completely lined with bookshelves. There were hundreds of books standing on the shelves. The room was cozy with warm colors of rust and bronze and cream. A large screen television filled one corner. Worn, chocolate brown leather armchairs faced it, along with a matching worn leather couch.

The pastor had walked over to a unit that housed a great selection of CD's and DVD's. While he was looking for the one he wanted, the pastor's wife sat down on the couch and patted the cushion next to her. The woman took her seat and waited.

It was a short wait. Making his selection, the pastor inserted the DVD and sat down in an armchair. A man came onto the screen introducing himself as Dr. Bernard Nathanson. He admitted that he had been personally involved in the performance of over 60,000 abortions, although now he was active in exposing the facts of this barbaric procedure.*

*From the video, *The Silent Scream*, 1984. Directed by: Jack Duane Dabner. Narrated by: Dr. Bernard Nathanson

As Dr. Nathanson showed the actual real time ultrasound of such an abortion, he told of a young doctor who had himself performed over 1,000 abortions. One particular abortion he was performing was being filmed via ultrasound and after the procedure, he was asked to watch and help edit the film. The young abortionist watched as the baby, who had been moving serenely while sucking his thumb, suddenly began to move about wildly. As the suction instrument he had used was inserted into the uterus, the baby made pathetic attempts to move away. The baby's heart rate increased rapidly to 200 beats per minute. The suction instrument grabbed at the legs, pulling them apart. At that moment the baby opened his mouth wide in what the doctor now believes to be a silent scream. Appalled, the abortionist left the room.

Moments later, having gained his composure, he returned to assist with editing, but he never performed another abortion. His attending nurse who had performed the ultrasound and was also present at the editing session was a strong feminist and pro-choice advocate. However, after seeing the results of the abortion on film, she resigned her position and never spoke about abortion again.

At one point in the narration, the pastor's wife reached over to take the woman's hand. The woman squeezed it, thankful for a comforting touch. The woman's eyes barely blinked as she watched the documentary. Surprisingly, she did not cry.

When the short film came to an end, the pastor picked up the remote control and turned off the television. He glanced at his wife and at the woman who was still staring at the television set. Then he sat back in his chair, stared at the ceiling, and waited; for what, he wasn't sure, but he waited.

After a few more moments, his wife let go of the woman's hand. This seemed to break a spell of sorts because the woman, who had been frozen in a trance-like stare, turned abruptly toward the pastor's wife and said, "My baby told me all that in the letter."

The pastor's wife felt her eyebrows lurch upwards. An expert at regaining composure or covering a shocked response, she said, "There was something in the letter about Dr. Nathanson and this video?" Her eyebrows had returned to an even appearance, but the surprise of the pastor's wife hadn't seemed to register with the woman sitting next to her, rigid, strangely without emotion.

"No," she answered, "not the video. My baby told me what happened the day he — or she — left me." Here she took a deep breath, then continued, once again in a trance-like stare. "My baby told me that he — or she — wanted to stay — tried to stay. My baby said, 'Something I never felt before came into my tummy house. I didn't know what it was, and I tried to get away. I was pushing with my feet. 'Mommy, did you feel me?' my baby asked.'"

The trance was broken here and the woman's face contorted into sheer torment. Tears welled in her eyes; her own mouth opened as if to scream, but made no sound. The woman, mouth open, eyes wild, sat motionless.

The pastor's wife, her own tears streaming down her face, moved close to the woman and wrapped her arms around her. This action seemed to break the woman's trance again. She fell into the pastor's wife's arms, crying violently.

The pastor also had tears in his eyes. He leaned forward, praying and wiping his eyes. His heart ached for the pitiful sight of this broken-hearted woman before him. How she needed Jesus to take away the pain. He prayed earnestly that the Holy Spirit would speak into her heart, letting her know how much God loved her no matter what she had done.

The minutes passed. Finally, there was nothing but silence in the room in the midst of a picture of one woman rocking another in her arms, and of a man bent forward with his head in his hands, his heart pleading in prayer for this woman. "Please God," he whispered in his heart, "show this woman how much you love her and want to help her."

More minutes passed. Then the woman sat upright, smiled tenderly at the pastor's wife, and mouthed a silent

"Thank you," while squeezing the kind wife's hand in her own. "I'm going to go now," she whispered, as if there were no strength to speak any louder. She stood. "Thank you for all your time. Thank you for — just for everything."

"You know where we are, my dear," said the pastor's wife. The woman nodded.

"Please don't hesitate to call if there is anything — anything we can do." The pastor spoke in earnest. Again the woman nodded.

Once more she said, "Thank you." Then, leaving the room, she walked down the hall, picked up her handbag and car keys from where she had left them on a chair in the dining room, made her way to the front door, opened it, and walked out into the night.

The pastor and his wife stood at the door. The woman did not look back. They said nothing more and closed the door.

"I'm so worried about her tonight," the pastor's wife said.

The pastor put his arm around his wife's waist and pulled her to him, holding her close in an effort to comfort her and also to comfort himself.

"Do you think she will be alright?" She asked.

"Literally, only God knows." he answered, but added, "One thing for certain, God will be watching over her in earnest."

"And loving her to Himself," the pastor's wife added. "Let's continue praying that she keeps her heart open to hear Him — to receive Him."

He kissed her on the forehead, took her hand, and led them both into the living room where they knelt side by side before God, pouring out their petitions for the troubled woman who had just left their home.

In the car driving home, the woman continued to feel a depth of pain that she had never known before. She marveled to herself that she was even able to drive, but somehow she found a determination to get home. She had to get home. To read the letter again? No. Not to read the letter. Well, not that letter. She wanted to read another letter; one that she had read as a child and had loved the stories it held. She wanted to find her Bible and read. What would she read? She didn't know and somehow it didn't matter. She just drove on with a resolve to read God's Words, believing He would show her what to read.

She pulled the car in front of her house, turned off the engine, and began walking up the path to her front door. The angels were watching. The Holy Spirit was moving. The truth of God's love was touching this woman.

THE RESPONSE

Once inside, she decided to take a shower before attempting anything else. Brain and body ached from all the crying, all the torment of the day. She needed to be physically refreshed. Yes, a hot shower was calling her name.

The water was streaming down, vigorously pelting her skin. She closed her eyes against the force of water, drenching her tear stained face, soothing swollen bags beneath reddened eyes. Then she turned and let the water pummel her back in delicious splendor. Oh, yes. This was good. The water, hot and hard, unknotted tensed up places. She felt a physical solace easing into muscles, alleviating some pain — at last.

Once dried off, and wet hair combed into order, the woman went into the living room and sank into the couch. She leaned back and took note of the clock on the wall: 11:20pm. What a long day, and it wasn't over yet.

The Bible. Where is it? She was certain she still had it — somewhere. She closed her eyes to think better. Where did she put it? The garage? Yes, probably the garage, where she keep rarely used items.

She walked into the kitchen, opened the door that led to the garage, and clicked on the light. What a mess! She had actually never had her car in the garage. Ever since she had moved in she told herself that she would get things into good order so she could actually use the garage for what it was meant — to house her car. So far she had failed.

She walked into the garage and stood there for several moments just staring at everything. "What a mess!" she wailed out loud. Then, with a small grimace lifting the left corner of her lips, she added, "It's a picture of my life — what a mess!"

"Now, where are those boxes?" She walked along the walls of the garage. There was her old bicycle from childhood. There was a broken microwave standing on a broken table. "Why haven't I taken that to the dump?" she asked herself out loud.

Two old lamps were stuffed into a cardboard box, the sides split from its oversized contents. A wooden stool, with a shoebox filled with little Christmas tree ornaments precariously perched atop it, stood in front of three stacked plastic boxes. A maze of cobwebs were attached to the legs of the stool. More cobwebs and dust were over the plastic boxes.

The woman went back inside and returned with a damp cloth and a broom. She knocked away the cobwebs from under the stool and carefully moved the stool and its shoebox cargo to one side.

Pulling one of the boxes to the floor, she opened it and found old college textbooks, old letters from college friends, and even some textbooks from high school days. She lifted one out. Political Science. She moaned. "Why does the world need political science? Politicians study it and still don't know what they're doing." She uttered a little laugh at her own joke.

She thumbed through another book called Classical Literature, lifted the heavy book titled Western Civilization, and there it was — her Bible. The cover was pink. That had been her favorite childhood color. The words 'Holy Bible' were etched in silver on the front. Beneath those words was written, also in silver, 'New King James Version'. The edges were bent and ragged in a few places.

Lifting the Bible out of the box, she sat right where she was on the cold concrete floor and opened the cover, turning a few pages until she came to it. She had remembered and wanted to read it again. The Bible had been a gift from her parents when she turned ten years old. Her father had written: "To our precious daughter. May the living words in this book lead you along good paths. May you always seek God's way. There is no greater joy. With all our love, Mom and Dad. Proverbs 3:5-6"

Her eyes lingered on the words from her father for several moments. Then a spark of excitement ignited her into action. She had wondered during her drive home where she would begin reading when she found her Bible. Now she knew! Her own father had led the way! Proverbs 3:5-6

She flipped through the Bible but couldn't find Proverbs. Then she located it in the table of contents. Excitedly she turned to Proverbs, Chapter 3. Scanning down several lines, she came to verses 5 and 6. She read out loud, *"Trust in the Lord with all your heart, and lean not on your own understanding; in all your ways acknowledge Him, and He shall direct your paths."*

The concrete floor had quickly become uncomfortable. She took her Bible back inside the house and sat down on the couch. That was much better.

She read the words of Proverbs 3:5-6 over and over. She thought if she read the words enough times, perhaps a secret code for living or for unravelling the key to inner peace would suddenly disclose itself to her. No such formula was revealed, so she decided to read down a few more verses. She read the next two verses — 7 and 8. *"Do not be wise in your own eyes; fear the Lord and depart from evil. It will be health to your flesh and strength to your bones."*

She stared out into nothingness as she tried to contemplate the meaning of the words. She had been wise in her own eyes — trying to figure out the best way all by herself. She didn't always choose the best way in life, but did anybody? Even the best of Christians must get it wrong sometimes. She pondered the notion further and admitted that, yes, Christians make mistakes, but they have God to let them know when they're on the wrong road; then He tells them the right road to get on.

Where did that explanation come from? She smiled softly. She remembered now. It came from her father. He had said that to a group of teenage boys he was teaching. She had sat on the stairs and listened from the hallway. When her father said those words, she remembered thinking how wonderful it was of God to help people when they got things wrong; how kind of Him to want to put them back onto the right path.

It was all coming back now. Suddenly she was remembering all sorts of things: words spoken by both her mother and her father, something their preacher said in a sermon, a lesson given by her Sunday school teacher. All these things — remembered — flooding back into her mind.

The brain is like a huge filing cabinet. She reflected on that thought, picturing her brain with all sorts of filing cabinets and hundreds of files with different headings. "How amazing is that," she declared out loud. "Surely, only an amazing God could create our brains like that."

She laughed then as she recalled something the pastor's wife had said to her that day. "What do you think, dear? Is it easier to believe that God created life or that an explosion created life?"

God created life. The woman's thoughts were emphatic; nothing wavering. Yes, it was a certainty. God created life. The woman began to feel — what? A slow release from the pain of the day? A touch of love to replace the grip of agony that had held her all day long? God created me, and He loves me, even with all my mess. He wants to forgive me. He can give me a new life.

A new life. Yes, her father used to quote a verse to his Bible class of teenage boys. What was the verse? Where was it found? She wrinkled her nose and squinted her eyes together, trying to think. A new life — a new life — old things gone away. Something like that. Where was it?

She couldn't recall and couldn't guess how to find it, but she remembered the gist of it. She remembered her father explaining to his boys that, when they let Jesus into their lives, their old life was gone; He gave them a new life.

She sighed with the welcome thought. Could she have a new life? Her baby has a new life. She would like to see her baby one day.

She smiled at the thought, and pulled a tissue from the box on the coffee table. Dabbing her eyes, wiping away the fresh tears, she knew that she wanted to see Jesus, too. She wanted to thank Him for taking care of her baby and for putting His happiness in her baby's heart. That's what the letter had said. 'In heaven everyone gets God's own happiness in their hearts.'

It was time. She knew it, and she wanted it. She bent forward, clasping her hands together and closing her eyes. "God," she began and paused before continuing, "I'm not sure exactly what to say, but I think I understand now. Like the pastor said, You love even me." She paused again, collecting her thoughts and then resumed. "Thank you for taking care of my baby. I'm so sorry now, God. I didn't know, but I never stopped to ask you, either. I never stopped to think about you. Will you forgive me?"

A wash of love, so pure and exquisite, gushed over her then. More of her own tears mingled with the love flooding the room, flooding her heart. This time her tears were of joy, such as she had never known. "Oh, thank you!" she cried, "thank you! Will you make me a new person now?" Even more love filled the room, enveloping her with sweet relief and yes — true happiness."

Lifting her face and opening her eyes, she smiled broadly. She couldn't remember feeling such love and peace. When had she truly been happy before? Compared to this, to what God had just put into her heart, no other earthly happiness compared.

"Oh God," she prayed again, this time her eyes open, looking up. "Thank you for your love. Thank you for forgiving even me. Help me to live like you want me to."

Abruptly she stopped praying and picked up her Bible which still lay open to Proverbs 3 and read verses 5 and 6 again, *"Trust in the Lord with all your heart, and lean not on your own understanding; in all your ways acknowledge Him, and He shall direct your paths."*

"God," she prayed again, "I don't ever want to choose my own way again. I'll mess things up. We both know that. Would you help me to know your path? I don't exactly know how that works — how you will show me, but I know you will. Thank you, again. Help me to live right. I can't do it by myself. Thank you." More love and more love and more love filled the room, permeating her heart with a fragrance of the beauty of forgiveness — of the beauty of Jesus.

She awoke to daylight and sat up on the couch. She didn't know when she had fallen asleep. She remembered such a beauty in the room; she had closed her eyes to better absorb it all. Now she was waking up.

It hadn't been a dream. She knew that for certain. Her Bible lay open on the coffee table, still turned to the book of Proverbs. A few crumpled tissues lay on the floor.

She ran her fingers through her tangled mass of hair. It felt like a bird's nest and probably looked like one, too. She sat there smiling.

It was a new day. Yesterday was the storm; today is the day of calm that follows. Reading that letter has had to be the hardest thing that I've ever done; she contemplated with a grimace at the memory of the pain. But without that pain, without having gone through the agony of it all, I would not be starting the first day of my new life! Her eyes glistened with tears of gratitude. "Thank you, Jesus," she whispered. "Thank you for letting my baby send that message." Instantly she sat straight up! The letter!

She ran to her bedroom. She wanted to get the letter that she had put back on her bedside table before going to the pastor's house. She wanted to put it in a safe place. She walked alongside the bed and stopped — there was no letter. She looked on the floor and glanced under the bed, even though in her heart she knew she would not find the letter.

She sat down on the bed, staring for several moments at the bedside table where the letter once lay. Had she dreamed the whole thing? Had she spent the whole of yesterday wandering about in a sort of hallucination?

As quickly as the troubling thoughts filled her mind, just as quickly they dissipated into sweet oblivion. The truth was — it didn't matter. Whether or not the letter had ever really been there, she knew the love of God had captured her heart. She desired to be a prisoner of such ecstasy forever. She would not turn away.

She had been forgiven of everything wrong she had ever done, and she had been given a life sentence. It was a sentence of destiny to live eternally with God in heaven — and with her baby, too. She sat smiling, basking in the sweet presence of God's love, for some time.

"My parents!" Her thoughts took a new turn as visions of her parent's delight came into her mind. She picked up the phone and punched in their number.

"Hello?" What a sweet voice her mother had. The woman had never really noticed before, but now the very sound was like music singing in her heart.

"Mom?" she began, "are you and Dad busy right now? I want to come and tell you something." There was a slight pause so the woman continued, "It's great news, Mom. I want to tell you and Dad in person."

"Of course. You come right over. We love good news," her mother chuckled into the phone.

"It's great news! I'm on my way!"

"I'll put the coffee on. Love you."

"I love you, too." The woman had always responded to her mother's signing off with love in a robotic fashion. Today the words she spoke back to her mother were heartfelt, deep, bursting with love.

The woman jumped into her clothes, pulled a comb through her tangled hair, and arranged it with clips toward the back of her head. She applied a dab of makeup, stood in front of her mirror for approval, and left the room.

Grabbing car keys and her purse, she headed out the front door, trotting down the walkway in her jubilation. A neighbor noticed her from across the street. He was out watering his grass.

"You're in a hurry," he called over. "Everything okay?"

"More than okay," she replied with a huge smile. "It's the best day of my life!" She waved as she got in her car, and pulled away, giving another wave to her perplexed neighbor. "Maybe someday soon I'll tell him what's happened to me." She was beaming with the thought. "Maybe I'll tell everybody!" She laughed out loud at the idea. The very notion of sharing with everyone she met suddenly filled her with a — a what? As she was mulling this over, it flashed into her mind — the very thought of sharing with others filled her with a sense of destiny.

She couldn't have known right then, but God had just called her to a lifetime of service. He was putting her on a path of His design. She had asked Him to choose the right path for her — so He did.

God loves putting His own desires into the hearts of His children. Those desires are always, without exception, filled with a joy that cannot be measured. Nothing this world has to offer can ever compare to walking the path of God's own design. It's a blueprint of purpose. It comes equipped with courage, inner peace, joy, and the sweetness of the presence of God with you. The woman would happily discover, over time, that indeed, there's nothing that can match the gladness of heart that comes from walking God's path.

THE PLAN UNRAVELED

Both her parents were at the door when she pulled up. She looked at them as she exited her car and smiled, feeling a tenderness toward them that she hadn't felt since she was a child. They smiled, too, always happy to see their girl.

"Come in. Come in," her mother chirped. "I've got the coffee on." The delicious aroma filled the air.

As she reached the door, she stepped in, first hugging her mother and then her father. Those hugs came from a heart of sincere love for her parents. The hugs were so affectionately given that her mother couldn't keep her eyes from shedding a tear, which she hastily wiped away.

"Your mother says you have some good news to tell." Her father's face was a picture of serenity. He always portrayed calm more than any other emotion.

"Not just good news, Mom and Dad, but great news!" She was looking from one to the other, her heart overflowing in her feelings of love and thankfulness for them. "You have to sit down." She walked through to the living room with them right at her heels.

She sat in an armchair. They took the couch. They sat smiling, waiting, anxious to share in their daughter's news.

"Mom and Dad," the woman began, "I know that you have prayed for me for years! Ever since I was born."

"Even before you were born," her Dad added with a quiet tenderness.

"Yes," agreed the woman. "I'm sure you did." Here she looked down at her hands, all of a sudden feeling ashamed at her past behavior towards her parents. These two sweet, sweet, loving people.

Her parents said nothing. They just waited to hear whatever it was their daughter wanted to share with them. She began again with, "I know I haven't been the best daughter."

Here her mother started to protest, but the woman stopped her. "Please, let me say what I must, Mom." The older woman smiled and nodded her head.

The woman continued, "I haven't been the best daughter because I somehow left God out of the picture." She paused again to collect her thoughts. She hadn't rehearsed what she would say, so her explanations, she felt, were all disjointed. Never mind. Determinedly she would plow on. After all, they would be delighted with her news.

Her mother had reached over to take her father's hand. She was subconsciously holding her breath, longing for a certain something to come out of her daughter's mouth.

"Yesterday — was a crazy, strange day." She paused again. Should she tell them about the letter? Maybe that was too much information for now. She would go right to the best part of her news. "I guess you could say God arranged to get my attention." She paused once more as she looked at her parents. Then, with a huge smile, and her eyes filling with tears, she blurted out, "Last night I asked God to forgive me and to come into my life. I asked Him to show me his path and to put me on it."

Her mother could not hold back the tears that flowed down her face. Her father wiped his eyes, too. The woman still had tears, even after yesterday. All three of them stood, moved toward each other and embraced.

When at last they let go of each other, her father said, "Hon, that is by far the best news I've heard in I don't know when." His eyes glistened in his happiness.

Her mother pulled a fresh tissue from her pocket and began wiping her eyes all over again. "I'm happier than I know how to say." She grabbed her daughter to hug her again.

The woman said, "I've never been happier, either. It took a while, but I finally got here." None of them could stop smiling.

Minutes later, they were all in the kitchen. Her mother was pouring delicious smelling coffee as her father sat down at the little kitchen table in the corner. The woman helped her mother bring the mugs of coffee to the table and sat down, too.

They sat there for a couple of hours, sharing together what was in their hearts. The woman told how she had talked with both the pastor and his wife. Although feeling saddened, she confessed the abortion she had had just months earlier. She couldn't look at her parents with this revelation, but when her mother took her hand in hers and squeezed it, she looked up into two faces of pure love.

"God forgives anything," her father said, "and nothing is ever wasted in His scheme of things. I reckon God has a plan to use this."

Something within the woman quickened. Her father's words were like God speaking to her. This was all new to her.

"Dad, hearing you say that I feel — it's hard to describe. I don't know if this sounds right but — it was like God

Himself speaking," she put her hand on her heart, "right into my heart."

"That sounds exactly like God to me," he assured her.

"One thing that stands for certain, God always uses things we go through to help someone else."

"Yes!" The woman exclaimed, excitement tingling up her spine. "I feel that, too! If I can help other women, then, maybe they won't make the same mistake I made — and maybe they'll come to know Jesus, too! Wouldn't that be wonderful?"

Her mother took her hand again, squeezing it in hers as she agreed with her daughter, "Yes, indeed. That would be wonderful."

The woman stayed with her parents the entire day. They talked and shared together, the parents reveling in their daughter's great news. After all, this was a day of anticipated celebration; the day they had prayed for, for so many years.

"Dad," the woman remembered about the verse she was trying to recall the night before. "Where is that verse that says something like, when we get a new life the old life is gone away? Is there a verse like that?"

"There sure is," her father answered with delight. "It's found in II Corinthians 5:17. It says, '*Therefore, if anyone is in Christ, he is a new creation; old things are passed away; behold, all things have become new.'*"

"Yes, that's it." The woman smiled in delight and repeated, "II Corinthians 5:17. I need to write that down." Her mother produced a pen and piece of paper. As she jotted down the Bible reference, she said to her father, "I don't know if you knew, but when I was a kid, I used to sit on the stairs and listen to you teach your teenage boy's class."

"I thought you were in bed asleep. You fooled me." He laughed, and added, "But I'm glad you did. I'm glad you heard the things of God that the boys and I discussed."

"Me, too. II Corinthians 5:17 is one of the verses I heard you explain to the boys. It obviously lodged itself in my mind because last night it came to me. Well, the gist of it came to me."

"God's Word never returns void," her mother spoke. The woman looked at her with a question on her face. Her mother explained, "That verse is found in Isaiah 55:11." She then quoted it: "'*So shall My word be that goes forth from My mouth; It shall not return to me void, but it shall accomplish what I please. And it shall prosper in the thing for which I sent it.*'"

"Wow!" The woman exclaimed as she picked up the pen and paper again, "I need to write that one down, too. This is so exciting!"

By the time late afternoon shadows were creeping across the lawn, the woman, at her parent's suggestion, had searched the Internet for training programs on dealing with women contemplating abortion.

"It never hurts to explore and have a look," her mother encouraged. The woman was, in fact, one who always made decisions quickly. She also loved the taste of adventure. Now she sensed she was on a new path — Gods' path — and wherever it would lead, it would be good; it would be meaningful, purposeful.

Within a couple of hours, the woman had chosen a nearby college that offered certificate and degree programs in counseling. She downloaded application forms. She also found and wrote down phone numbers and addresses of pro-life organizations. It seemed clear to her that she needed training in counseling. Perhaps, too, she could volunteer in some capacity at a pro-life center.

The woman stayed for dinner. Her parents were delighted with her visit. They could not remember the last time she had spent so much time with them. Now with her newfound faith in God, they could share on a level they had never shared before.

When the dishes were washed, dried, and put away, the three of them sat together on the back porch. There was time to enjoy a frothing mug of hot chocolate before saying goodnight to each other.

It was only a quarter moon, but its wash of soft, white light graced the lawn in its luster. A gentle breeze was moving about the leaves of an oak tree which stood tall and majestic at the end of the yard.

"This is all a beautiful sight, isn't it?" The woman's face held a glow that matched the shimmer on the lawn, her smile bathed in tranquility.

"Yes, what an amazing Creator God we have," her father shared in his daughter's appreciation of the nature displayed before her.

"Your father and I often sit out here in the evenings, enjoying the beauty of the outdoors," her mother added. She said with a laugh, "It's the same sight every night, but we love it all over again every time."

The woman smiled. Yes, she could imagine her parents never tiring of anything that God had made. They had always had such gratefulness for everything about God. I want to be like that, she thought, with a determination behind the feeling. Yes, she would aim for that goal.

It finally came time to say good-night. Her parents followed her to the front door and hugged again, speaking more words of joy for her discovery of the love of God, for her invitation for God to come into her life.

Waving good-bye, she pulled away from the curb and started for home. A lot had happened in 48 hours. She let out a sigh of contentment. "Old things are passed away," she said out loud, as a huge smile formed on her lips.

That same smile was still there when she arrived home. She was tired — deliciously so — but she had just one more thing to do before she got herself ready for bed. She picked up her phone.

"Oh, my dear!" exclaimed the pastor's wife, "thank you so much for telling us. We have continued in prayer for you all day! Oh, what joy!"

The woman heard her call out to her husband, "Our prayers are answered with joy!"

"She's asked Jesus into her life?" The woman heard the excited pastor's voice call out from the distance, his wife answering a jubilant, "Yes! Yes!"

The woman thanked them again for the amount of time they had given to her. She thanked them for sharing in her grief. Most of all, she thanked them for putting her on a path to understanding.

Now she was ready for bed. She showered, crawled beneath the covers, lay her head on the pillow, and closed her eyes. Sweet sleep.

In heaven, the angels were still rejoicing as they do when just one who was lost — is suddenly found.

THE TRAINING

Several Years Later

The woman completed her training in counseling. It had not been an easy road. She juggled college assignments with her job, volunteered at a local pro-life organization, and in time, taught a group of teenage girls at her church.

It wasn't easy; not only because of the heavy load of responsibility she carried with college, her job, and church, but working hard to keep her own emotions on a Godly track. She learned early on in her walk with God that Satan was not happy with her decision. He had failed in attempts to keep her from giving her life to God; therefore, all he could do now was to try to keep her from walking close to Him.

He did this on a constant basis. Some days the woman felt strong. She would remember to turn to God immediately, using His own words to thwart off the evil enemy. Once, she had even shouted out, like Jesus had done, "Get thee behind me, Satan!"

Other days, like Eve in the Garden of Eden, she would take time to consider what he said. That was always a big mistake. She found that listening to the enemy was a joy killer! He was always accusing. He would remind her of her past failures. Worst of all, he would constantly tell her that she was a murderer. She had killed her baby and the results were irreversible. She could not clear her mind of his accusations.

At such times, listening and considering what the enemy had told her, she would sink into a depression. That, too, made her feel a failure. Surely, she would reprimand herself, she must take God's own courage. It was available to her. Therefore, she concluded, the devil was right. She was a failure for letting weakness overcome her inner spirit, sucking her down into a quagmire of guilt and despair.

Her self-accusing tirade would sometimes continue for days or even weeks at a time. It was then, added to her already depressive state, that she would feel pangs of conscience for hypocrisy. Everyone sees me as some kind of wonderful, Christian person. They see me as a sort of hero for helping young girls and women who have become pregnant but don't really want to be.

In fact, people did see her as a lovely, gentle lady who loved God deeply. They thought her brave and full of Godly compassion. Some even thought her to be wise. When those accolades would come her way, she would inwardly cringe, especially if she were presently suffering a bout of depression and self-condemnation. It was hypocritical. "I'm a fake!" she would often shout at the mirror, loathing the woman looking back at her.

In the early days of her Christianity, she suffered bouts of depression and self-loathing on a regular basis. She had to admit, with the passing of some years, she had matured to the point that she knew to quickly get help. Waiting around, hiding herself beneath piles of bed covers, trying to sleep away the doom and gloom that clutched at her mind, had never helped. She knew it never would.

Eventually, she became more astute at detecting the first signs of the enemy's attack. She would phone her pastor or his wife, who were always ready to help. God had given them such wisdom. They always seemed to have just the right verse to share with her, or they would pray such a prayer over her that it would plunge down, like an anchor in perilous waters, bringing her stability and steadfastness.

At such uplifting moments, she would remember, too, to treat her troubled soul. Our physical wounds are treated with particular medicines, she often told herself. Therefore, our spiritual or emotional wounds must be treated with particular medicines, also. For her, when despair would damage her inner tranquility, she would listen to music. It was like a balm soothing unseen places with healing.

It wasn't just any music. It was songs of praise to Jesus. It was songs about His love. It was songs about the Holy Spirit washing over her with truth and compassion, strength and peace.

Music concentrated her thoughts on the truth and love of God, helping her to better focus and recognize the lies of the enemy. When in the realms of healing music, she could stand strong against any lie; against any accusation the enemy threw at her.

Sometimes she thought about David. He was her favorite Bible hero. He, too, had been a murderer. He had committed adultery. He had lied and deceived. He had done all that after being used by God to defeat the giant Goliath. How could one so close to God fall so far away?

The woman often recalled a particular conversation she had with her father. She loved discussing Bible truths with him. He was so wise. He had such insight, explaining in simple to understand words the deep truths of God. In this conversation they had talked about several Bible characters, but they had come back to David, as they so often did. The woman felt she could identify with David.

"David had been tempted," her father told her. "There is no sin in being tempted; it's what you do with the temptation that can land you in trouble." He had gone on to explain that, "David left God out of his actions. He made his own plan. Therefore, he ended up on a terrible path that led him to adultery, murder, and an awful attempt at cover-up."

"It's amazing, isn't it, Dad," she had said, "that God forgives anything."

"Oh, yes," he had agreed with a contemplating look on his face. "Wonderfully and amazingly, the vastness of God's love covers and forgives anything. I love the verse in Isaiah 1:18 that says, '*No matter how deep the stain of your sins, I can remove it. I can make you as clean as freshly fallen snow.*' But," he continued in earnest, "there must be true repentance."

"Yes," she had nodded her head in total agreement and added, "one must always say I'm sorry."

"And?" Her father had prompted.

Lines on the bridge of her nose crinkled in uncertainty. "And…" Her eyes darted here and there, revealing her baffled mind. "Umm — oh! Of course!" She slapped the palm of one hand to her forehead. "One doesn't just say 'I'm sorry,' but also asks to be forgiven." She looked pleased with herself.

"No," her father had said matter-of-factly. Smiling at her astonishment, he went on to explain, "Many Christians make the mistake of thinking that if they say they are sorry and ask forgiveness, then they have repented and all is well. But that isn't repentance."

The woman had leaned forward, drinking in the words of her father. She knew this was going to be good; she was not disappointed.

"Repentance means to turn away," her father told her. "In the original Greek, the word for repent is *metanoia.* The literal translation is 'to think differently after.' It implies a change of both mind and heart. Do you understand?" he asked her.

"I'm getting there; continue please," she answered.

"When we become aware that we have sinned, then we take on a humble attitude. That attitude doesn't just say, 'please forgive me,' and then goes out to purposely commit the sin all over again. To repent is to resolve not to do it anymore. You purpose in your heart that you don't want to do it again, and you ask the Holy Spirit to remind you of this fact."

He had watched his daughter mulling over the truths he had just shared with her. He never tired of her questions about the things of God. It had been a longing in his heart to talk this way with his daughter for a very long time. What a joy it now was to watch her in her thirst for more and more of God in her life.

In the coming years, the woman also met criticism, sometimes severely, from those who opposed her position that life begins at conception. No one likes criticism, and she was no exception. On a few occasions, that criticism had even shown itself in the form of abusive email and text messages. She had changed her phone number three times now as a result.

Interestingly enough, she was able to shed the after effects of these attacks rather quickly. Although shaken at the onset, she would instantly remind herself that the people attacking her were as confused with it all as she had once been. She, too, had been unsettled, ambiguous, and angry. She had been an emotional wreck. Therefore, she maintained that others needed the same compassion and patience that she had been given during her own days of grief and suffering.

Sometimes, too, she met pro-life people who seemed to be full of hate for those holding to a pro-choice view. It was understandable, in her mind, if the angry people were not Christians. However, if they were Christians and behaved in an unloving manner, it saddened her to the core of her being.

"Do you think that's what Jesus would do?" she had asked a group of people who were making placards with large letters that spelled — MURDERERS! "Don't you remember the story of the woman caught in adultery? It was the custom of the day to kill her for this sin. What did Jesus say to them? He said, 'Okay, kill her, but only those who have not sinned may throw the stones.'"

The group had stood silent. The woman continued. "The same is true today because God's truth never changes. His love and truth are our only constants in this world."

Still, the group stood silent. The woman said, "I once aborted my child. Yes, I murdered my baby. If you had come at me with these cards," she held up one for all to see, "I would have been filled with anger and hate toward all of you. I would not have considered your viewpoint at all."

By now, several heads were lowered in shame.

"Do you know what got my attention? It was a few people, pro-life people, who showed compassion and love to me.

They explained when life begins — but they did it through arms holding me in love, not accusation."

By now a few people had put their placards aside. The woman was filled with continued boldness. She heard herself give a plea. "I'm actually wondering if you truly understand the real meaning of Christianity. If there is anyone here who, like me, was once a very angry person and who, like me, would like to consider Jesus, then I would be happy to talk with you. You see, anyone can have Jesus, and He sure makes the world of difference; He is amazingly real. For me — well — He made my life worth living." She smiled here, softly, genuinely. Then she left the room and went to the office where she had some paperwork waiting.

A man and a woman suddenly appeared in her doorway. "Hi," the man spoke. "This is my wife. We were both touched by what you said." He looked at his wife who nodded encouragement to her husband. He continued. "We would — we would like to know about Jesus. You make Him sound so..."

"Relevant," his wife interjected.

"Yes. I — we — always thought Jesus as sort of, well, old fashioned, but you make Him sound, like my wife said — relevant — for today."

"Come in," the woman smiled, indicating two chairs in front of her desk. She rose, closed the door, and proceeded to lead them to Jesus. They were ready. They were seeking real meaning to life, and they found it — in Jesus.

Later that same afternoon, the woman stopped by her parent's house to share the events of the day. They loved their daughter's frequent visits. Their hearts were as one now. What a difference that made.

"Who would have thought," the woman was saying, while she accepted a mug of steaming, black coffee, "that one day I would not only be a Christian myself, but I would have opportunities to lead others to Jesus? It's amazing!"

"And who would have thought," her mother joined in, "that not only would you be a Christian and bringing others to Jesus, but you would have grown to be such a leader among your peers."

"What?" Her daughter appeared stunned at this statement.

"You do know what a leader you are, don't you?" Her mother asked, equally as stunned at her daughter's reaction.

"Well..." The woman had absolutely no words to say.

Breaking into a moment of hearty laughter, her father said, "You didn't even see it coming your way, did you?" At this he laughed again, but continued, "That's probably one of the attributes that God sought and found in you — a humble person just going about her business, never contemplating leadership. You see, God has actually been training you all along the way. Everything, I mean, *everything* that you have been involved in was being used by God to mold you into the leader that He planned for you to be."

The woman was still speechless. She parted her lips as if to speak, but no sound escaped her mouth. She was a leader? How did she not see that happening?

Her father went on, saying, "For many years, I have been aware of people, usually in the church, who speak out loudly that God has called them to be a leader. They seek positions, nearly *demanding* a role, because they are insistent that God has called them to lead." He paused here to take a sip of coffee before continuing. "The only problem I found with their declarations of leadership was the fact that no one was following them."

The woman smiled. Her father was not a man of many words, but when he spoke, it was best to listen because something of value was about to come out of his mouth. This nugget of human observation was a gold piece.

"I see what you're saying," the woman spoke, a warm feeling of love all over her.

"Thank you," she said, looking at both her parents. "Thank you for what you see in me."

"It's not only us," her mother said with a smile of pride. "Others have told us what a strong and wise leader God has made you."

"God's anointing on you is obvious," her father stated with a look of sheer joy.

"Wow." The woman hardly knew what to say next. "I guess people do follow me. They want to talk to me, to ask my opinions — even my advice. It's the same at work or at the pro-life center or at church. I guess I do carry quite a bit of responsibility, and people do look for my direction." She laughed here as she said, "Who would have ever thought?"

Draining her mug of coffee, she set it down and said, "Wish I could stay longer, but some teens from my class at church are coming over. We're having pizza and a movie at my place tonight."

"You all have a great time, Hon." Her mother rose as her daughter stood. She gave her a hug and a kiss on the cheek. "Love you so much, Hon, more than you know."

"Thanks, Mom. Love you both, too, more than you know."

As his daughter left the room, her father reminisced briefly, recalling the years and the tears that he and his wife bore on their daughter's behalf. At times, their grief and concern over her life's choices left deep wounds of sorrow. But her coming to Christ had healed those wounds.

He got up and poured more coffee. He sipped and smiled as his reflections took him back to the night of despair that God had turned into hope and confidence. Their daughter had announced her engagement to someone who was not a Christian. Adding to that unsettling news was the fact that they would move in together before their marriage. Her attitude had been haughty as she informed them of her plans. It was almost as if she both dared them and longed for them to argue and fight with her. They did not take the bait.

When she had left their home that night, his wife cried deep and heavy, while he felt he could barely breathe; his chest heavy and painful. He had not told his wife at the time, but he speculated he might be having a heart attack. He had leaned back in his chair, closed his eyes, and made silent cries to God, begging for His strength to get them through this latest devastation. When would their daughter see that any road without God would ultimately lead to ruin? Would she ever know that life with Him was filled with all sorts of never-ending adventure?

It was on that night of overwhelming heartache that he and his wife had made what they called their Declaration of Care before God. They had stayed up all night discussing and praying. He was in the middle of his recollections when his wife returned from seeing their daughter off.

"Are you alright? You look troubled." She came nearer to inspect her husband. "You're pale."

"No, no, I'm fine. I was miles away, though. I was remembering." He held out his hand, and she put hers in his. He pulled her down to sit in the chair next to him. "I was recalling," he told her, "the night of our Declaration of Care."

"Oh." She said nothing more for several moments and then, "I've shared that several times over the years."

"You have?" He seemed surprised.

"You don't mind, do you?" She asked with a little apprehension in her voice.

"No, no, of course not," he assured his wife as he patted her hand. "I've shared it, too, with a couple of men I work with who had the same concerns for their children."

"Did they do it? The Declaration of Care? The ladies I shared with all did it, and it brought strength and peace to every one of them."

Her husband smiled, then chuckled, "That's wonderful. The men I shared with also did it, and it helped them, too. I wonder why we never told each other."

His wife reflected on this for a moment and then answered, "It's a private thing. It was private for us. Maybe we were each respecting the privacy of our friends and their troubles."

He smiled and agreed, "Yes, that's probably right." Going back again in his thoughts to that night he said, "It was a hard night. We could see our baby girl deliberately making a choice that she knew was against the things of God."

"Yes," agreed his wife, "it was one of the most painful memories I have to this day." They were both quiet for several minutes.

"Do you think the pregnancy is what led to the broken engagement and then to the abortion?" she asked.

"I don't know. It seems it could have been. I've never wanted to ask."

"Perhaps she has never said anything about why the engagement ended because, well, because it's no longer important to her now. Perhaps she just never thinks about it." His wife smiled as she shared her theory.

"You may be right, and if so, isn't that wonderful?" His eyes were shining now as he added, "That would be just like God to make something that had been so painful come to a sweet place of inner healing."

They sat together, sharing more moments of companionable silence. Then, taking his wife's hand again, he said, "You know, you have shared the Declaration of Care, and I have shared the Declaration of Care. We both can testify that it has brought peace and courage and hope to those who have tried it."

"Yes?" His wife felt waves of excitement ripple through her. "What are you thinking?" she asked, her face a picture of giddy anticipation.

"I'm thinking," he stroked his chin and leaned in toward his wife. "I'm thinking — maybe we should..." He paused again. His wife could barely stand it.

"What? Say it! I think I've got the same idea going through my mind!" She clasped her hands together like a little child about to receive candy.

Her husband laughed out loud and said, "I think we should share it with the pastor. Maybe this would help other Christian parents. There are so many who are heartbroken over their children because they are wandering through life with no regard for God."

His wife clapped her hands together, nearly shouting, "Yes! That's what I thought!" She leaned forward and embraced her husband. "God sure arranges some surprising things."

"Yes, indeed," her husband agreed. "Life with God is one adventure after another. It's walking into the unknown, and it can be scary, but when God Himself is leading the way —"

"It promises to be a great journey." His wife joined him in that last phrase. "I've heard it before," she said with a smile, "from a very wise man called my husband."

He kissed her on the forehead. Then he went to the phone and called the pastor.

THE DECLARATION OF CARE

The pastor, and his wife, too, had immediately warmed to the idea. After that initial phone call, they had met in the pastor's office where he listened attentively to how God had impressed on the hearts of this man and his wife to make a Declaration of Care regarding their one-time wayward daughter.

Two weeks later they were enjoying a meal together. The purpose of this get-together was to pray for God's leading and then to talk about the way forward. The two couples were aware of the presence of God in their discussion. For this they were thankful, as they would not have proceeded if they did not sense His blessings on the plan.

"Have you discussed this with your daughter?" The pastor asked.

"Oh yes," answered the mother. "We had never told her before how we had made our pact with God, so to speak. When we told her what we had done, she hugged us, thanked us, and told us how much it meant to her."

"Then," the father said, "She took us out to dinner!" They all laughed, sharing the joy in the results of the Declaration of Care that they had made with God.

The mother added, "She told us that when we got started, if we would like her to, she would be happy to come and share her testimony, encouraging other parents and showing them that she is an example of why not to give up."

"What an excellent idea," agreed the pastor.

"Sounds just like her," the pastor's wife said.

Within a few more weeks, they had put words on paper and had them printed into small booklets. Then the pastor shared the plan in church. It was also advertised on the church's website. Responses began to pour into the church office via emails and phone calls.

"Looks like we'll have nearly 40 parents coming to the first meeting," the pastor talked excitedly into the phone. "Are you still willing to come and give your testimony?"

"I'm very happy to come," the woman replied. "If other parents can see the outcome of prayer and trust in God — well — it has to be good."

"Indeed it does," agreed the pastor. When he hung up the phone, he took time to have a little talk with God, thanking Him for all He had done in this woman's life. How broken she had been; how beautifully He had remade her.

In two weeks, the first session of The Declaration of Care met together. The woman was there, ready to give her testimony. After the pastor briefly welcomed everyone, the woman's parents took the stage.

"We are here tonight with our lovely daughter." Her parents smiled at her. How blessed she was to have had parents who never stopped praying for her or loving her, no matter what. What a beautiful picture of the love of God being made evident in the lives of His children.

"She already knows about everything we are going to share tonight. You see," her father was in his element, talking about how God changes lives, always for the better. "We could say that she is the star of this meeting, but we won't say that because, if we did, our daughter would quickly remind us that it's God who is the only star here."

The group responded in applause. Their faces were pictures of grief hidden behind smiles. There was a dullness in the eyes of many. No doubt, they came with huge burdens, wondering if perhaps they might find hope here.

The woman began to pray in her heart that the Holy Spirit would touch hurting hearts, filling them with reminders of the promises of God. She prayed that they would understand that when our hurts are placed in the hands of God, it frees Him to do His perfect work of healing and changing. He heals broken hearts. He changes lives, removing the old and making all things new.

She finished her prayer. Then she began listening attentively to her father. He was explaining the Declaration of Care that he and her mother had developed before God.

"On one particular night, when our daughter told us of her plans to marry, we were heartbroken. The man she intended to take as her husband was not only an unbeliever, he was — well — we're being honest here, right?" Heads nodded.

"He was just not a nice man. Our daughter deserved better. We could see it." He looked at his daughter as he said, "She could not. It was like she was blinded to the obvious." He was still looking at his daughter. She smiled and nodded her agreement with all he was saying.

Her mother then took the microphone. "Our daughter had shown no interest in the things of God since she went to college. We prayed regularly for her, but it was that desperate moment when she announced her engagement that brought us to make our Declaration of Care before

God. Oh, was it ever wonderful to have done so! You see, with our Declaration we came to know that not only could we trust God to deal rightly with our daughter, but we could trust Him to take away our pain — our torment."

The woman noticed several people leaning forward; their body language clearly saying that they were identifying with her hurt and longing for her hope. The woman prayed again. She asked the Holy Spirit to keep their minds attentive to all that they were hearing tonight. She asked that they would have faith to believe — to at least try. She knew that Satan would not be pleased with what was going on here tonight.

"It was in the midst of many tears," her mother shared, "that God Himself put into our hearts the challenge of The Declaration of Care. My husband will now explain exactly what that is. I know that's what you're waiting for." There were a few smiles. She added before handing the microphone over to her husband, "You won't be disappointed."

"On that night of our daughter's engagement announcement, we felt like a balloon with all the air let out. In our spirits, we were flattened to despair, but — and this is key — we thank the Lord that we still had stamina and fortitude to pray. We just began to pour out our hearts to God. As we were crying out to Him, telling Him how we felt and how scared we were for our daughter, a sweet presence came over us. It was the presence of God Almighty." His wife was nodding her agreement.

The woman wiped a single tear from her eye. The pastor and his wife were rejoicing in their hearts at what God had done. The people who had come with hearts breaking were now sensing possibility in places where hope had been dashed to pieces.

Her father continued, "The Holy Spirit brought us some vastly important reminders. By the way, that's why it's important to study God's Word. At times when you need comfort and guidance the most, the Holy Spirit can bring back to your memory those things you once read and studied. It's like planting seeds. If you don't plant, of a certainty, nothing will grow."

The woman smiled. She had heard her father use that illustration over the years. He had told his teenage boy's class all those years ago. He was still telling people. That's because God's truths are never changing. They are pillars in any difficulty, anchors in any storm.

Now she heard her father sharing the points of the Declaration of Care. Even though she knew what was coming, she, too, was leaning forward in anticipation. She smiled with pride in both her parents. They had endured so much. They were giant stalwarts of the faith.

Her father began, "These are the points that the Holy Spirit brought to our minds:

FOCUS - Keep Looking Godward

1. Why stay focused on God? Because He cares deeply for you.

"Casting all your care *upon Him, for He* cares *for you."* I Peter 5:7

•The word 'care' is the Greek word *merimnah* meaning worry or anxiety.

•The word 'cares' is the Greek word *melo* meaning to pay attention to or to take interest in.

Therefore, never forget that your Heavenly Father is giving you His attention. Never forget that He is taking an interest in you — in all the things that worry you.

2. Why stay focused on God? Because He will hold you up, supporting you with His own strength.

"Cast *your burden on the Lord, and He shall* sustain *you; He shall never permit the righteous to be* moved." Psalm 55:22

•The Hebrew word for 'cast' is *shawlak* meaning to throw away or to hurl to one side.
•The Hebrew word for 'sustain' is *kul* meaning to provide for or to maintain.
•The Hebrew word for 'moved' is mowt meaning to be shaken or to totter.

Therefore, never forget that as you determine to throw your worries onto your Heavenly Father, He will then provide everything you need to get through anything that causes you to be anxious and troubled. His own strength will keep you from being shaken in fear or from tottering on the edge of worry.

ACTION PLAN - Planting Seeds

1. What seeds do we plant? The seeds are the very Word of God.

"...the seed is the Word of God." Luke 8:11

In this chapter, Jesus gives an illustration called a parable, which is a story that reveals hidden truth. He talks about the conditions of a person's heart, which is like soil. When the seeds land on good soil — they will grow.

2. Planting seeds isn't just all talk. Talk without action is ineffective.

"My little children, let us not love in word or in tongue, but in deed and in truth." I John 3:18

3. It will be the demonstration of love for your children who are not walking with God that will prepare their hearts to be good soil.

"By this shall all men know that you are my disciples, if you have love for one another." John 13:35

4. Speak God's Word as opportunities present themselves.

"And you shall know the truth, and the truth shall make you free." John 8:32

5. Encourage yourselves with the fact that as much as you love your children, God loves them more.

"The Lord...is not willing that any should perish, but that all should come to repentance." II Peter 3:9

6. Planting seeds of God's word is most important for parents of young children.

> *"Train up a child in the way he should go, and when he is old, he will not depart from it."* Proverbs 22:6

This verse is often misunderstood, causing many parents to feel like God has not kept His Word. They tell themselves that they raised their children in the things of God, but their children, now adults, are not following God. In other words, according to their understanding, this verse is not true because their child departed from the training to walk in the ways of God.

This is not at all what this verse is teaching. If it were, in fact, it would be nullifying the free choice God gives to each person. God will not force anyone, even those raised in Christian homes, to follow His ways.

So, what does the verse mean? It's all to do with planting seeds. If as parents, you train up your children in the ways of God by planting seeds of God's truth in their hearts, then when they are adults those seeds are still there. The *seeds* will not depart.

As you continue to love and to pray for your wayward adult children, the hope is that their hearts will be fertilized by your love and prayers. This fertilization will help to make the soil of the heart ready to produce the fruit of the seeds that are already there. The seeds can now grow in the ways of God.

For those of you who, for all sorts of reasons, did not train up your child in the ways of God — perhaps you weren't yet Christians yourselves — don't lose heart here. A most important verse to stand on is Luke 1:37, *"For with God, nothing shall be impossible."*

In other words, it's never too late to begin planting seeds of God's love in someone's heart. It's never too late to plant words of God's truth. Seek those opportunities. Ask the Holy Spirit to make you aware and to help you to fertilize your adult child's heart in love. Ask the Holy Spirit to make the soil of the heart ready for the seeds of God's truth to grow. It's not at all impossible; quite the contrary, because all things are possible with God in the midst.

PETITIONS - Pray For All The Above

Our efforts can produce good things, but our best attempts at anything are still only second best without the anointing of God. Therefore, do not make attempts out of the goodness of your own heart; but rather, go forth in the power of the Holy Spirit. Surrender your concerns, cares, troubles, and worries to God; let Him take over. Pray to keep yourself walking in the ways of God. Then the seeds you plant in your children will come from a heart of God's love and not just from your own concern.

PRAY FOR THE FOLLOWING:

1. That you remember every day to cast your cares on God.

2. That you trust His love for your child.

3. That your child's heart will develop good soil where planted seeds may grow.

4. That seeds planted will be fertilized.

5. That you recognize opportunities to show love and to speak God's truth as God leads you to do so.

GIVE PRAISES TO GOD FOR THE FOLLOWING:

1. That He has your and your children's best interests in His own heart.

2. That He gives you His own strength to sustain you; to be your Everything, through anything.

3. That He is not willing that anyone die without knowing Him. He desires everyone to choose His perfect way of love, joy, and peace.

4. That He gives you opportunities to show His love and to speak His truth.

5. That He gives you blessings every day of your life. Take time to list those blessings.

6. That He has shown you the way of repentance and salvation.

GUARD YOUR HEART

Satan will not be happy that you have chosen to embark on this Declaration of Care. Therefore, it is essential that you guard your own hearts from the wiles of the enemy and the cares of this world.

"Above all else, guard your heart, for it affects everything you do." Proverbs 4:23

When our heart is not strong in the things of God, it affects our decisions, our Christian walk, our relationships, and our commitment to pray. Daily be aware of the enemy's possible attacks. Remember, Satan is strong, but our God is stronger, and the Spirit of God is within us.

The woman's father stopped here and asked, "Is this clear to everyone?"

Heads nodded.

"If not, don't hesitate to seek me out and ask me to explain it further. I will be happy to do so."

He looked over at his wife, motioned for her to come closer, and handed her the microphone. She smiled at her husband, took the microphone and said, "We have a booklet for each of you that covers everything my husband just told you."

Someone in the group called out, "Oh, thank you! That was a lot of material, and I knew my brain couldn't retain it all."

This was followed by good-natured laughter. Then someone else said, "What you and your husband have put together sounds — well — like it came right from the Lord." Murmurs of agreement followed.

The woman watched her mother, so confident, so respected by others. She wished she had always seen it. What wasted years! Stop it! She chided herself. Yesterday is gone; today, as my Dad once reminded me, God is restoring that which the locusts destroyed. She smiled. She loved that promise found in Joel 2:25,

"The Lord says, 'I will give you back what you lost to the stripping locusts, the cutting locusts, the swarming locusts, and the hopping locusts. It was I who sent this great destroying army against you. Once again, you will have all the food you want, and you will praise the Lord your God, who does these miracles for you.'"

Her father had explained to her that God sending the locusts was Him allowing pain and misery and using it to bring His people back to Himself. Then, in His vast love, He restored that which had been lost. She sighed. I have today, and today I'm so proud of and thankful for my Mom. Love has blossomed between us. Yes, the woman reflected, the enemy spoiled many years yesterday, but God is restoring them today.

Her mother was telling the group, "We would like you to arrange yourselves in groups of four. You will be in these groups throughout our sessions together. Every time we meet, we will break into our groups where we can share with each other the concerns we have for our children. Bring a notepad so you can write down the names of the children in your group. Pray for each other."

There were murmurs of agreement. A spirit of excitement was in the air.

Her mother continued, "Every week, before we break into our groups, we will have a time of worship in song to keep us praising. We will then have a time of teaching from God's Word to keep us focused. Following the Word, we will have our group discussions and prayer times."

She smiled broadly as she finished. "When we acknowledge God's Word, worship and praise Him for who He is and all He does for us, and then bow our hearts together in prayer — the devil doesn't stand a chance!"

There were shouts of "Praise the Lord! Hallelujah! Thank you, Jesus!"

Then the group broke out into raucous laughter as someone called out, "Go on back to hell, devil; there's no room for you here!" There was definitely an aroma of holy confidence in God sending its fragrance into the hearts of all present.

"There is one final thing to share about our sessions together," her mother instructed. "You will see at the back of your booklets that there is a verbal pledge that we will make before God and before each other. My husband and I spoke it out loud together when we began The Declaration of Care. Would you like to have a look at it now?"

When her mother saw that everyone had found their places, she read the following:

"**We declare** that we know God loves us and cares deeply for us.

We declare that the moment we recognize worry in our lives, we will turn to our Father because He cares deeply for us.

We declare that we give the care of our children to God because He cares deeply for them.

We declare that we know when seeds of God's love and of His Word are planted in the hearts of our children, the seeds are there to stay.

We declare that we will pray every day for our children to understand the vastness of God's love and care for them.

We declare that God's promises are true all the time. We trust Him. We give our hopes and our concerns to Him because we know He cares for us.

We declare that we will guard our hearts from attacks of the enemy, and we will maintain our focus on our Father. It is He who cares for us."

As her mother turned to go, the woman's father came back to take the microphone. He paused, then said, "It is my great joy, to introduce to you, the one by whom the Lord made our Declaration of Care possible. Please welcome our wonderful daughter who has come to love Jesus so very much." Her father's voice cracked, and he wiped away a tear.

The woman drew in a quick breath and held it, lest she begin to cry. She walked to the stage, stepped up onto the platform and into the arms of her waiting father. Cheers and great applause filled the room.

"I'm so very happy that each of you have come here tonight," she began. "Everyone here has a different story to tell — but the worries for your children will be the same. I assure you, God's plan to love each one to Himself is the same, too."

Amens were heard around the room. All eyes were glued to this woman. She represented hope of what their children could be too, with Jesus in their lives.

"I was raised in a Christian home, but when I left that home to find my own way, I left without any thought for God's way. I know now that my parents were more heartbroken than I could have ever imagined then." Here she glanced at her parents. They smiled their encouragement to her. "Those seeds that have been referred to several times tonight were planted in my heart. Those seeds have always been with me." Heads were nodding. Hearts were being gladdened. "However, it took a terrific anguish in my life to bring me to God. What I went through —," the woman took a deep breath here, "— I would not wish on anyone. "Nevertheless," she quickly added, "going through that torment was worth it all; it opened my eyes to the beauty of God's love for me."

At this point, the woman removed the microphone from the stand and stepped out from behind the podium. She moved toward the audience. She wanted to be close to them. She willed them to comprehend through her story that there is hope for each of their stories, too; for with God, nothing is impossible.

She told them about her career climb at work. She told them how she feigned happiness, but deep inside, when she could face herself, she knew something was missing. There was a recognizable void.

She told them about her childhood days when, after being put to bed, she would sneak downstairs, sit on the step, and listen to her father talking with his class of teenage boys. "The words of God that he spoke to those boys," she explained, "were seeds being planted in my own heart. When I was in the midst of my greatest trauma, it was those seeds, and seeds I recalled from my Sunday School teacher and my pastor at that time, that suddenly began to grow in my heart. You see," she took another step closer to the audience, "all along, those seeds had been watered in love by my parents. If that had not been done — well — maybe I wouldn't be standing here today."

A few women were wiping their eyes. Her parents were wiping their eyes, too. All faces expressed their own identification with the woman before them. All of them were sensing hope.

"I encourage you," the woman continued, a strength in her every word, "never give up. Giving up is what Satan wants you to do. Instead, go God's way. That's what Satan never wants you to do. You know who cares for you. You know who holds your every concern in His own heart."

The woman paused here, taking time to look at each person, smiling her encouragements to them. Then she asked, "Will you keep planting seeds and watering them with love no matter how long it takes? Can you trust your Heavenly Father to love and care for your children, even more than you do?"

There was only a split second of a silence. Then the entire room of hurting parents stood to their feet. They were answering out loud, "Yes! Yes! Yes!" More tears fell; but this time they were mingled with hope and relief, easing away pain.

In the coming weeks, months, and even years, this and other groups of people came to know the sweetness of their Father's presence with them always. They better understood His love and His care for them in all their concerns. Many of their children came to know Jesus; others did not — yet. The parents never gave up. They remained focused on God, swimming in the floods of His peace that washed over them. Trust in their Father grew. Therefore, in the midst of all their pain, steadfast joy grew, too.

CONCLUSION

Are you someone contemplating abortion? Have you already had an abortion? Help is always found in Jesus, and He is always waiting to pour His love into all our hurting places. He can give you hope and a future.

If you would like to talk to someone about Jesus, I encourage you to seek help from a local pastor or from a committed Christian that you may know.

In addition, you may go to the following website which specializes in helping women gain emotional and spiritual healing, specifically in the area of abortion.

www.silentnomoreawareness.org

Other helpful websites are:

www.rachelsvineyard.org
www.healinghearts.org
www.ramahinternational.org
www.JenniferONeill.com

Are you a parent, heartbroken over a child who has chosen a path without God? I hope you seriously consider trying The Declaration of Care. Your Heavenly Father truly cares for you and your loved ones. He is paying attention to your worries, holding your interests in His own heart. He can be your strength in any storm.

If you have been touched by this book, it is my prayer that you *"run with endurance, the race that God has set before us...keeping your eyes on Jesus, on whom our faith depends, from start to finish." Hebrews 12:2-3*

Dr. Vickie J. Blair

Other Books By Vickie J Blair

1. With Wings Like An Eagle
   God's Work In Kyrgyzstan

2. Back On The Potter's Wheel
   An Autobiography of Spiritual Discovery

3. A Year Not Wanted
   When Blessings Come In Crisis

4. Developing Your Spiritual Eyesight
   A Weekly Devotional For Individual or Group Study

5. Avoiding Shipwreck
   Keeping Faith Strong

For Young Readers 12+

6. The Great Cascade
   An Allegorical journey

For Children 2 - 6 yrs.

7. Molly Moo and Her Hair-Raising, Frightful, Very Scary Day

8. Grandpa Rooster and His Silver Treasure Chest

By Chuck Blair

Reflections Of The Tabernacle In The New Testament

Made in the USA
Columbia, SC
03 November 2022